The
Canary
Islander

Barrie Mahoney worked as a teacher and head teacher in the south west of England, and then became a school inspector in England and Wales. A new life and career as a newspaper reporter in Spain's Costa Blanca led to him launching and editing an English language newspaper in the Canary Islands. Barrie's books include novels in 'The Prior's Hill Chronicles' series, as well as books for expats in the 'Letters from the Atlantic' series, which give an amusing and reflective view of life abroad.

Barrie writes regular columns for newspapers and magazines in Spain, Portugal, Ireland, Australia, South Africa, Canada, UK and the USA. He also designs websites to promote the Canary Islands and living and working abroad, and is often asked to contribute to radio programmes about expat life.

Visit the author's websites:

http://barriemahoney.com
http://thecanaryislander.com

Other books by Barrie Mahoney

Journeys & Jigsaws (The Canary Islander Publishing) 2013
ISBN: 978-0957544475 (Paperback and eBook)

Threads and Threats (The Canary Islander Publishing) 2013
ISBN: 978-0992767105 (Paperback and eBook)

Letters from the Atlantic (The Canary Islander Publishing) 2013
ISBN: 978-0992767136 (Paperback and eBook)

Living the Dream (The Canary Islander Publishing) 2015
ISBN: 978-0992767198 (Paperback and eBook)

Expat Survival (The Canary Islander Publishing) 2015
ISBN: 978-0992767167 (Paperback and eBook)

Message in a Bottle (The Canary Islander Publishing) 2016
ISBN: 978-0995602700 (Paperback and eBook)

Escape to the Sun (The Canary Islander Publishing) 2016
ISBN: 978-0957544444 (Paperback and eBook)

Expat Voice (The Canary Islander Publishing) 2014
ISBN: 978-0992767174 (Paperback and eBook)

Island in the Sun (The Canary Islander Publishing) 2015
ISBN: 978-0992767181 (Paperback and eBook)

Footprints in the Sand (The Canary Islander Publishing) 2016 ISBN: 978-0995602717 (Paperback and eBook)

Living in Spain and the Canary Islands (The Canary Islander Publishing) 2017 ISBN: 978-0995602724 (Paperback and eBook)

Letters from the Canary Islands and Spain (The Canary Islander Publishing) 2018 ISBN: 978-0995602731 (Paperback and eBook)

Secrets and Lies

Barrie Mahoney

The Canary Islander Publishing

The
Canary
Islander

Acknowledgements

I would like to thank all those people that I have met on my journey to where I am now and to my partner, David, for his love and support, as well as for his proof-reading skills.

To the children in the many schools where I have worked as a teacher and inspector, for their laughter, optimism, openness and natural insight into life.

To professional colleagues in schools throughout England and Wales, whose skill and dedication I have been privileged to witness and have so often admired.

Disclaimer

This book is a work of fiction, and the places and characters mentioned are fictional, and not based on any actual place or person living or passed away.

Dedication

This novel is dedicated to David, my life partner, without whose love, support and encouragement this book would never have been written.

Contents

Three Years Later …

Prologue

It was late morning and the sun continued to bake the small township with its unrelenting heat. The township lay in a dusty ravine, and despite a few clouds in the brilliant blue sky, it was an airless day and everything seemed as dry as dust. A few dogs were barking in the distance, the occasional rider stopping outside the store, and then tethering his horse before escaping from the heat. There was an air of dreaded expectancy in the township; this was the day that they had been waiting for, and dreading. It was the day when Big Jake was due in town, and the stench of death was already in the air.

The saloon bar was busy. It seemed as if the townsfolk sensed that there was safety in numbers, or maybe it was just an unspoken wish that they should all spend their last day together. The bartender looked nervously at the clock on the wall. It would soon be time. He started nervously stacking away the empty glasses beneath the bar, and removing bottles from the shelves behind him.

The thunder of horses' hooves entering the small township made the townsfolk feel uneasy. Those that were outside scuttled into the saloon, or back to their homes to escape the coming tensions and ultimate showdown. A cloud of dust appeared in the distance, as horses and riders reached the outskirts of this quiet town. A small boy stood transfixed outside the General Store.

The air was heavy with expectation. The birds stopped singing, and the gentle neighing of horses resting outside the blacksmith stopped, as they too shuffled their hooves nervously. There came a thunderous sound, as a group of six horses and their riders burst into the village like a hurricane. The leader of the group, a big, fat unshaven man with heavy sideburns and moustache, leapt from his horse.

"Where is the little runt? I'll put a bullet through anyone I finds hiding him here! Do yer hear me!"

Any townsfolk that were watching the entry of Jake and his pose of criminals suddenly melted away. They disappeared into homes, shops or anywhere they would not be noticed. The small boy continued watching by the door of the General Store. No-one seemed to notice him, or be concerned about his safety.

"I knows you're all in there!" Jake bawled through the door of the salon. "You got five seconds to hand him over, or me and my mates will blow up the whole building - with you lot inside!"

"There's no threatening going on in my town Mister," came a voice from outside the Sheriff's office. The Sheriff, a tall, burley man, wandered to the group of riders with a gun in hand "You throw your gun down, and walk over here, real quiet. We got you covered, so you comes real quietly."

The Sheriff fell to the ground as a well-placed bullet shot through his head and he fell to the dusty ground. There were screams from some of the women watching through the windows and doors of the saloon bar. The small boy watched, with no expression on his young face.

"Right. That's a taster of what my men's gonna do to all of you unless you hand him over. Me and my men will shoot all of you, and raise this miserable town to ashes. You got another five seconds."

"Five, four, three, two..."

"I'm here Jake. Don't touch these people. It's not their fault. They are innocent of my crimes. Just let them all go in peace. I'm over here," came a voice from the roof of the General Store.

"Ah, you's seen sense at last, Blondie. Just come over here to your Uncle Jake. I gotta surprise for you!" boomed the big man.

A slim, blonde young man, slipped down from the roof of the General Store, with the ease and grace of a gymnast. He walked slowly to his tormentor, as the townsfolk once again began to appear from their doorways. They watched in awe at the grace and composure of the handsome young man with the long blond hair. The townsfolk began to clap, as he slowly approached Jake.

"Strip the little runt," ordered Jake. "Check him for sudden surprises. You know what happened last time. This one likes to play games, don't you Blondie? This time, there'll be no escaping, as its time to meet your maker!"

Two of the five remaining men grabbed the young man and roughly ripped off his dusty jacket, blood stained shirt, trousers and worn boots. The young man was left standing in nothing more than his grubby grey pants. The crowd watched in silence as they caught sight of this handsome, yet defiant stranger standing in their midst. He was someone that they had accepted and welcomed into their small community. They knew what would happen next. The small boy began to shake and then to sob loudly. Jake walked over to the terrified child, cuffed him with the back of his hand, and the small boy stumbled.

"Don't you dare hit the kid! You pick a fight with me, but not the kid. That's the coward's way, Jake, and you knows it! You leave him alone."

Jake hit the terrified boy yet again, but this time harder and with the edge of his gun. The terrified child cried and fell to the ground. Jake kicked and spat at him, as he wandered over to the young man whose hands and feet were now bound with coarse rope.

"I'll do want I want with that bloody kid, after I've finished with you! You can either tell me where you stashed it and I'll blow your brains out real quick, or you can stay silent and I'll blow your balls off - and wait a while before I blow your brains out. Either ways, it's not gonna be a pretty sight," snarled Jake.

The young man said nothing. He stood defiantly glaring at the man who was about to take his life away, There were was one shot, together with long pause as the young man fell to the ground and writhed and screamed in agony. The second shot brought peace, and silenced the screams as the beautiful young man with the bright blonde hair fell to the ground, surrounded by a pool of blood.

Chapter 1

"James, James, wake up!" whispered Christian urgently into the ear of his sleeping partner. "You're having a bad dream, Jay, wake up!"

"Don't hurt him! Don't hurt him! Let him live. Let me look after you. I love you!" shouted James, who was by now shaking and kicking his legs violently. After a few seconds, the tension ceased, relaxed breathing resumed and James slowly opened his eyes. He lay silent for a few moments, as if trying to resume entry to another, more familiar world.

Christian held his partner tightly, caressing him in his arms and gently stroking the long dark brown hair that lay on his pillow. He kissed James gently on the lips.

"You're having the same nightmare again, aren't you?" asked Christian gently. "Would you like me to get you a cup of tea?"

"No, not yet. Just hold me. I'll feel better soon."

" Is it the same nightmare as you usually have?"

James nodded. "Yes, exactly the same. It's so vivid. It is in the same place. Everything is the same. I can even smell and taste it. I don't understand what's happening. Dreams and nightmares, yes, but why the same one, playing like a record over and over again?"

"Tris is in the exactly the same trouble each time I guess?"

James nodded. "Yes, it's always the same. The same people, the same words, the same cruelty, over and over again." He paused and looked at Christian.

"Look Chris, I know I've said this so many times before, but it's you I love. I love you more and more with each day that we spend together. It just seems so wrong dreaming about Tris. He died long ago. It must be so hurtful for you."

Christian held James tightly in his strong arms.

"Look Jay, we've talked about this many times. I understand your love for Tristan. I loved him too remember? He was such a special person. Everyone loved him and it was so cruel that he left us all so tragically. He may have died a long time ago, but we all still think about him, talk about him and wonder what might have been. He made such an impression on the lives of all who met him. I don't expect you to ever forget him. You must never forget him. I do have one question though. Are you sure that the character in the dream is Tristan. It's not ..."

"No, it's not Sam, if that's what you are asking," snapped James. "I know my Tris. That Sam was a fraud, an impostor. He nearly ruined our lives and he very nearly killed Prince. Yes, I know they looked alike, but Sam has no heart, no soul. I hated him so much. He nearly destroyed us all."

"Well, maybe you did hate him, but they were so alike in many ways. I just wondered ..."

"Yes, I know what you mean. I may have flirted with the idea of Sam being a kind of replacement Tris, before I really got to know what a psycho he was. He was nothing like the generous, funny, crazy, loveable, angelic Tris that we all knew and loved. Yes, I did feel sorry for Sam Rivers at one time, and I guess I was nearly taken in by him, and all his promises. There's no doubt he's a very gifted gymnast, as well as gifted con artist, but he's ruthless. He's out of our lives now and you've been brilliant about it, but that was well over five years ago. Why I am still in such a mess about it all?"

"Well, to be fair, it's only been the last few months that you have had these nightmares, isn't it? Maybe you should have a chat with the Doc again, and change the medication? Maybe those pills are doing you more harm than good?"

"All Doc Emerson tells me is to relax? Me, relax? It's like telling a tiger to become a vegetarian!"

"Hmm, yes, I do see what you mean," laughed Christian. "Look, maybe it's the job that's triggering all these problems? Such a lot is happening now and I know how much you have put into it and the village. Don't underestimate the effect it may be having on you. Maybe, just maybe it's time for a change? A new job in another area? A fresh start? I'm sure I could get a transfer to another branch if I asked."

James sat up in bed, looking horrified. "Oh no, not yet! I should hate to leave the school and village, and I would miss everyone, especially Doris and Lotitia; they have all become our extended family. They have been so good to both of us over the years. I shall never forget how kind they were to me when Tris died. I thought my life was at an end, and then you came along."

"And Prince, don't forget Prince. He's the real hero of the place," laughed James, pointing to the large, fluffy dog who lay snoring loudly at the end of their bed. "I tell you if that dog gets any bigger, we're going to have to get a bigger bed. By the way, did you bath him as you promised the other day? He smells really bad again."

"That's true," laughed Christian. "I don't know why he has a basket; he never uses it. As for the bad smell, Lotitia let him swim in her duck pond again just after I had bathed him, so you can blame her. Yes, Prior's Hill is a very special place, isn't it? I seem to have been accepted as your partner and no one in the village ever questions us being together any more. We have so many friends here, and we seem to be accepted as a couple. I never thought this would happen in our lifetime."

"Yes, we have been very fortunate and Prior's Hill is a very special place. Don't forget what a bad time Jasmine and Paula are having in town. It sounds as if they'll eventually manage to get rid of her from the library. That tribunal is giving her so much worry, but they are determined to get rid of her. After all, do you really think our Jasmine would try to grope that woman in the nonfiction section? It's all a huge misunderstanding, and has been blown up out of all proportion. You know how over the top Jasmine can be? Anyway, she's devoted to Paula. Thank goodness

Paula is standing by her. Jas was so upset when I went to see her the other day. She was crying so much that I had to give her a cuddle."

"You did what? Oh God, James, not again! Is she still on about you fathering a kid for them? Is she still offering you the real thing or the test tube option?" laughed Christian.

"Ha ha! I reckon you're jealous Mister," teased James. "Just because she regards me as a perfect specimen of a man to father their kid, with my piercing blue eyes, firm jaw line, fine physique, dark brown hair, massive intelligence and ..."

"and great modesty!" laughed Christian, before trying to smother a giggling James with a pillow.

Chapter 2

A bleary-eyed James peered around the door of the kitchen. "I'm so sorry, Chris. I know you wanted an early start this morning, but I fell asleep again."

Christian poured a steaming mug of black coffee, which he handed to James. "Don't worry about it, Jay. I know you are exhausted and really needed to sleep in this weekend. It's a nuisance that we have to go on a long journey today, but I really do need to find out more. That letter sounded urgent."

James sat on a stool, sipping his coffee and nodded. "Where's Prince? He leapt off the bed when you left. He is usually around here hoovering up toast crumbs."

"All sorted. I took him over to Doris this morning. She loves having him, and I didn't think it was fair for him to be sitting in the car for such a long journey."

James grinned. "So how did you manage that? I thought there was always a right old battle as to who has Prince. Lotitia seems determined to spoil her hero whenever she can. I'm surprised that Doris had a look-in this time. Lotitia can be so determined when she wants to be."

"She can, but so can I. I simply told her that Prince had a severe tummy upset after she let him swim in her pond the other day, and I wanted him to spend the day quietly indoors. She certainly didn't want Prince to be throwing up over her Indian carpets, so she didn't argue. She does adore him though, but he did save her life."

James laughed, "Well, I'm pleased you did it. I'd never have got away with it. You know what Lotitia is like when she wants something."

"I do, but I'm not about to be bossed about by the gentry, as you often are, Jay. They'd suck us completely into their world if we'd let them."

"I know, I know. My goodness, you are becoming quite the revolutionary nowadays, Chris! You didn't used to be like this when I first met you."

"Ah, but then I wasn't politically educated before I fell in love with my favourite headteacher, was I?" laughed Christian, hugging James. "Look, we ought to soon be off. Do you want toast or something?"

"No, I'm OK, coffee is fine. Maybe we can stop for something on the way. I'm looking forward to taking the Spitfire out for a long drive again. Since Prince arrived, we don't seem to use it very much when we go out."

Christian groaned. "Oh no, Jay. I don't think I can stick a long journey to Cornwall in that. It's a great little car, and I know you love it, but it ruins my back every time I ride in it. Please let's take the Escort. I'll drive there and back, I promise!"

James tried to looked shocked and disappointed, "OK, OK, it's a deal, but only if you drive, because I will just drop off to sleep."

"Yes, I know you are exhausted, but you did spend nearly all of the first week of the holiday working in school. You should have had some time off to relax. Now you are heading into the Autumn term with flat batteries. You are not looking after yourself; I do keep telling you. Let's make sure we use the rest of the summer relaxing and enjoying ourselves."

"I know, but with the extension, new teachers and another couple of classes to set up, there's a lot to do. Someone has to be on site each day to keep an eye on those builders."

"It didn't have to be you every day, did it?" argued Christian. "You need some time off. We hardly saw you all week. Anyway, I'm sure Anne and Cedric would help if you asked them?"

"I'm sorry, I'll try to do better during the rest of summer holidays, Chris. I'll have a word with Anne when I see her. Let's get this show on the road. Remind me, what are we doing and why?"

Christian sat down on a stool opposite James. "Look, as I tried to explain yesterday, I had this weird letter from a woman, a Mrs Viers, who claims that she is my aunt, half cousin or something. I have never met her, but I do remember my mother talking about some old girl living in Cornwall. I thought she was dead, but maybe this is the same woman. She says that she has to sell her cottage, because she has to go into a home. She knows I'm an estate agent, and wants me to give her some idea of price, and that sort of thing."

"Couldn't she get a valuation locally? You've got a branch down there. Seems a bit much dragging us all that way just for that."

"I know, what you mean, Jay, but I just felt a mixture of curiosity and something weird. You know my feelings; they rarely let me down."

"I know you and your feelings, Chris," laughed James. "Come on, let's get on with it. The sooner we go, the sooner we can be home and can collect Prince. You know that Doris will want us to stay for a meal when we get back?"

Christian grinned, "I know, that's what I'm banking on. It's my turn to cook!"

Almost as soon as the boys had left Lavender Cottage, which had been their home for the last three years, and had turned out of Coombe village, Christian noticed that James had dropped off to sleep again. Christian often marvelled at James' seemingly endless abundance of energy, but there were times when he was concerned about him. In many ways, James drove himself far too hard, and at cost to his own health. He would struggle through school terms only to fall sick with a heavy cold or flu at the beginning of each school holiday. Christian had tried hard, but he couldn't get James to adapt to a sensible home and work life balance. James loved his school and Prior's Hill village; in turn everyone knew and loved James, but it was taking a toll on his health and occasionally their relationship; sometimes Christian felt that he was merely a bystander in James' life.

As he drove, Christian Trill reflected on the tumultuous three years that they had shared together. As the manager of a local estate agency, Whitney and Walker, Christian was familiar with all the comings and goings in the area; businesses that were doing well, businesses that were failing, marriages, divorces, births and deaths, schools, and those people who made any community what it was, were all of interest to Christian in his professional life.

Christian was well aware of the popularity of the young man sleeping in the car seat beside him within the community, and the love and respect shown towards him. Their relationship had not been easy. Any relationship has its problems from time to time, but a relationship between a gay couple, and particularly those in high profile and professional jobs, always caused eyebrows to be raised, particularly within a small community. James Young was now at the stage that he simply didn't care what others thought about him. He had a passion for his school, education and the lives of the young people in his care. That was all that mattered to him, that is until he met Christian Trill.

Christian knew that he had met the man that he would spend the rest of his life with. They had created a comfortable home in Lavender Cottage, but Christian often wondered if it was time to encourage James to move to another school - maybe one with a lighter load? After all, he had received plenty of suggestions from both County Hall and the Diocese, but James had always tossed the suggestion aside, saying that the time was not right. It was true in many ways; James had dragged a small failing school into one of the most popular and well-respected schools in the county. It had rapidly expanded its number of pupils on roll, which was why a significant amount of money was being spent on new classrooms and other improvements, which James was determined to see through.

"Do you want me to take over driving for a bit?" mumbled James, waking slightly and realising that Christian had driven for a long time.

"No thanks, Jay. You rest and I'll let you know when we are nearly there, and give you time to wake up. We will soon be heading on to the moors, which is always a lovely experience, if it isn't raining."

"It always rains on Bodmin Moor. Probably a good reason not to have brought the Spitfire today; the soft top is not as waterproof as it should be."

"That's the least of my worries with that car," thought Christian. He loved to tease James about the car, but he knew that it meant a lot to him. The 1967 vintage Triumph Spitfire had been belonged to Simon, James' late brother, who adored the car that he had bought from new. James had promised to look after it, after his brother was diagnosed with a terminal illness and could no longer drive. James had kept his promise, and the car looked as good as new, since it was usually kept in a garage under a dust sheet. The Spitfire was rarely driven, until Christian came into James' life and insisted that he use it regularly, at least on his drive to school. Even so, two young men and a large dog were not very well suited to such a small sports car. Christian was pleased that he had recently, but reluctantly, exchanged his elderly Ford Escort, which was often the subject of James' jokes, for a much newer model. Christian glanced at James slumped in the passenger seat; he was asleep again.

"We are just entering the village James, so maybe you should wake up now", said Christian giving James a hearty poke.

"That was a quicker journey than I thought," mumbled James slowly waking from a deep sleep. "It's not raining either, which is a change. I don't think I've ever seen the moors without rain. I used to work in Cornwall, you know. I often used to come walking out here."

"Really? I didn't know that. That must have been a long time ago. I don't think you have mentioned it before."

"It was when I was a student at training college. I came on a hiking holiday with a group of lads, but we ran out of money. I managed to get a job in a local pub and ended up working as a barman for the rest of the holiday. It was good fun and I learned a lot about people doing that job."

"Wow! You actually had a normal job and were not Mr Headmaster all your life," laughed Christian. "I'm very impressed. Actually, I could really see you as a barman. You are very good at chatting to people."

"Well, I was very good at it," agreed James. "I was quite good at making cocktails too, when I had the chance, but there wasn't a huge demand for them locally. To be accurate, my main job was pot washing and mopping out the toilets. Anyway, I made some money for the summer. It got me away from my folks, and I managed to get some walking done on the moors, when I had some time off. I enjoyed that summer."

"So, you can relax then? We must make sure we do this again, Jay. Prince would love walks here and it might force you to actually relax."

"Maybe, just as soon as that extension …"

Christian interrupted the flow of the conversation, since he knew what was coming, and he had heard the same conversation many times before, "Just follow the map for me. I've marked where the cottage stood be. We should be quite close now. Apparently, 'Hope Cottage' is quite a way outside the village, and at the edge of some farm buildings."

Chapter 3

The name 'Hope Cottage' was scruffily painted on top of the rotting gate, which Christian carefully opened. The crazy paved pathway and adjoining garden was covered with a variety of tall weeds, which led to a whitewashed building that looked little more than an outhouse than someone's home. The windows were rotten and the little paint that was still applied was peeling badly. Christian knocked on the green painted door, which was slightly ajar. "Anyone in? It's James and Christian to see you, Mrs Viers."

"Remind me, what is our relationship to each other?" asked Christian, after he and James had made their introductions to the elderly woman who was sitting upright in the wheelchair before them. The old lady was slightly built, with a firm, determined chin. Her long, wispy white hair was carelessly tied and pushed to one side of her gaunt, pale face. A large woollen blanket covered her knees. Another large, comfortable chair was at her side; other than this, the small room was barely furnished.

"Great aunt, cousin, whatever," snapped the old woman. "It doesn't really matter. The point is, we are some kind of relatives. I knew your mother, Christian, many years ago, and she told me that I could always count on you."

"I don't understand," began Christian, "How did my mother know you? She has never mentioned working here, or you for that matter."

"Who said it was here?" snapped Connie Viers. "I never said it was here. Did I say it was here? Did I say it was here, Connor?" she repeated, addressing the question to a small boy who was writing on small unpolished table in the corner of the dark room.

The small boy turned around, "I don't think so, Gran," he replied, before turning back and continuing with his writing.

"I'm so sorry, I didn't see you there …" began James, addressing the small boy.

"Doesn't matter, you're here to see me and not him," snapped Connie Viers.

"Even so, manners cost nothing," says James, walking across to the boy. "As the boy is in the room and party to our conversation, I think we should at least introduce each other. I'm Mr Young, what is your name?"

The small boy turned to face James, stood, bowed slightly, and held out his hand. "Good afternoon, Mr Young. My name is Connor. It is a pleasure to meet you. I hope you have had a good journey."

"Good to meet you too, Connor. This is my partner, Christian. Yes, we had a good journey, thank you, although I think I was asleep for most of the way."

"Bodmin Moor is very beautiful at this time of the year, Mr Young. It's a pity to miss its beauty by sleeping."

"Never mind all this chit chat," interrupted Connie. "You are here to see me and not to chat to the boy. Now this is the problem …"

"Ah yes," interrupted Christian, fearing that James would take offence at the interruption. "I think you wanted to ask me to value your cottage. Now, from what I can see, and you will understand that at this stage, it is only provisional. I will need to see the rest of the property before I can come to a conclusion."

"Stuff and nonsense!" interrupted Connie. "I didn't ask you to come here for that. I don't own the property anyway, it's rented. What I really want you here for is to take Conor home with you."

There was a pause, as this critical piece of information became clear to both Christian and James.

"Er, pardon. What did you say? You want us to take Connor home with us?"

"Correct," nodded the old woman. "That wasn't too hard to understand was it?"

"Just a moment," began James. "You ask us all the way here to value your property, which you don't own, but instead ask us to take your grandson home with us? I'm assuming he is your grandson?"

"Correct," snapped Connie. "My goodness, it takes time for you two to understand a simple problem, doesn't it? It's all quite clear. My daughter, Connor's mother, died some years ago. I took him in, but as

33

you can see, I am quite sick myself and I cannot continue to look after him. This is where you two come in."

"Hold on," started Christian, "What do you mean that this is where we come in? I don't know who you are, we have never met, and we cannot take the boy, which I am sure is illegal anyway. Connor may not want to come with us; he doesn't know us. It's an awful thing that you are asking us to do."

"Don't be such a wimp, boy. Your mother said you would always help me out, and I need help now. Simple, isn't it?"

"I really don't think we should be talking like this, in front of Connor," began James. "It isn't right. Anyway, what about his father?"

"Father? Father? What about his father? He ain't got no father! I guess he had one once, but I don't know who he is, my daughter never told me and Connor has never met him, have you boy?" shouted Connie Viers, turning to Connor who once again turned away from his writing and shook his head.

"Not that I'm aware of Gran. I'm sure I had one, but I've never met him."

"There you go!" triumphed the old woman. "You've heard what he said. There ain't no mother, there ain't no father, and there soon won't be a grandmother. I'm dying."

Christian eventually spoke. "Hmm, I'm sorry to hear that, but surely social services can help you if you are unwell."

"Can't you bloody well get it?" yelled Connie angrily. "There is no one, and social services don't care. All they do is sit in their posh offices all day. There's only you. After all, you are a relative and I'm bloody owed it."

"Owed it?" exploded James. "Please don't swear in front of Connor. What do you mean by owed it?"

"I looked after Christian's mother, and gave her money when she was ill. She said Christian would look after me when I needed it, that's all."

"This is crazy," began Christian, looking at James. "I know nothing about any of this. I don't know you. I've never heard of this from my mother, who conveniently for you passed away some time ago. We cannot possibly look after Connor."

Connie spoke with forced clarity and at a slow speed to express her wishes, as she lifted herself out of the wheelchair, with considerable effort. "Well, if you don't take him, Connor will be all alone in the world. I'm going into hospital tomorrow, and I doubt I will ever return. If you don't take him, he will be all alone here, and you will have that on your consciences if he dies and is eaten rats!"

"Oh, don't be so dramatic, woman," said James, firmly. "Look, we will look after Connor for a few weeks, as you ask, but then we will bring him back to you when you return from hospital. Which hospital is it, so we can find out how you are getting on?"

"St Agnes, Bodmin. By the way, that's his case packed over by the door."

Chapter 4

The journey home to Coombe was an awkward one. This time, James was driving, and it was Christian who was doing his best to make polite conversation with Connor, who sat bolt upright in the back seat staring blankly out of the window. There was no expression in his face, just a blank, wide-eyed stare on his emaciated face. Christian felt desperately sorry for the boy, who had been suddenly uprooted from his home and his grandmother, and was now heading somewhere new with two men he did not know. Christian felt both uncomfortable about the situation they had all found themselves in, as well as deep sadness for Connor. He tried to start a conversation, but the response from Connor was either a simple "Yes, Christian" or "No, Christian."

Once they had crossed the Moor and were back on the main road home, Christian once again tried to strike up a conversation.

"We have a dog waiting for us at home. He is called Prince, and is a wonderful, brave dog who has had some amazing adventures. I'll tell you about them one day. Do you like dogs, Connor?"

"Oh yes, I love dogs. I love all animals," replied Connor, sounding interested for the first time since they had left 'Hope Cottage'. I had a dog when I was little, but she was very old and died. I was very upset."

Christian nodded, "Yes, it's horrible when they die, but I'm sure she had a happy life with you. They live on a different time line, if you know what I mean?"

"Oh yes, I do," replied Connor. "I've sometimes thought about it like that. I like cats too."

"So do I," began Christian, "I used to have one as a child. Did you have a pet cat too?"

"No, not really. There was a cat on the farm near the cottage, and she had kittens. The farmer said I could have one. There was a lovely little black and white, tiny kitten, which I loved the first time that I saw him. I think it was because he was a bit like me. I took him home, but Gran wouldn't let me have him and I had to take him back. She said it wasn't fair to keep him, as we couldn't afford to feed him properly and anyway, we would be moving again soon. I called him Mittens, because he had four white paws."

"Oh no, I'm sorry to hear that. You gave him a lovely name though," said Christian. "Why did you think he was like you?"

"Oh, the farmer called him the runt of the litter and was going to drown him; that's what my Gran sometimes calls me. Just because I'm a bit small for my age."

"That's not a very nice thing to say, is it?" began Christian. "We're all different sizes and shapes, it's what's inside you that matters. How old are you Connor?"

"I'm nine, but Gran says I look like a six-year-old. I don't know why I'm small, but as I said, I'm like Mittens."

"I'm pretty sure if we could see that kitten in the next year or two, he would be growing into a big, fine cat. Just as you will be one day, Connor. Don't you worry about that. Er, I don't mean that you will grow into a big fine cat, Connor; anyway, you know what I mean."

Connor gave a faint smile and nodded.

Meanwhile James, who was driving, sat in silence, focussing both upon the road, as well as the conversation that was going on between Christian and Connor. The boy was certainly small for a nine-year-old, but he was as articulate as a young teenager. He had a voice of amazing clarity; he was well spoken and had a wide vocabulary, which James had rarely come across in someone so young.

James was also very troubled. Surely, what they were doing was against the law? They were taking a child away from his home and grandmother without any written agreement from anyone. Connor was clearly undernourished, and his sickly, white pallor was indicative of someone who was rarely exposed to sunlight and fresh air. This boy needed a healthy diet and lifestyle. What had they got themselves into?

"Anyone hungry?" exclaimed Christian.

No one answered. James was far too busy considering what to do to think about food, and there was no response or interest shown by Connor.

"I'm starving. I haven't eaten since breakfast, What about you Connor? When did you eat last?" asked Christian with slightly forced enthusiasm.

"I'm not sure. I think it was yesterday sometime. I had a sandwich that the farmer gave me when I went to see the kittens."

James winced when he heard this. "Didn't you have a cooked meal at all yesterday or anything today?

"No, Mr Young, we didn't have anything in. Gran said we would be leaving, so there was no point in buying any food."

"Did Gran cook for you when you had some food in?" asked Christian.

"No, I cooked usually. The gas stove didn't work. Gran was never very well and couldn't stand up for long. We had sandwiches a lot. I like making sandwiches."

"I think we need to stop for a meal as soon as possible, Christian," began James. "I think there's a Little Chef somewhere along this road. We could stop there for a meal. I don't think it's a good idea to go to see Doris tonight, but one of us should go to collect Prince and tell Doris what is happening."

"Good idea. Yes, I agree. The last thing we need now are lots of questions; first we need a plan."

A few minutes later, James, Christian and Connor stopped at a busy 'Little Chef' roadside restaurant. Initially reluctant to eat anything other than a cheese sandwich, Connor finally agreed to join James and Christian by ordering an omelette and chips, which he clearly enjoyed. Connor also happily accepted a glass of milk and a large piece of chocolate cake. He ate quickly, and without a word until he had finished. He sighed, looking satisfied, wiping the crumbs off his mouth with the sleeve of his grubby shirt."

"That's the best meal I've ever had!" he exclaimed with a slight smile.

"We're pleased you enjoyed it. I see you like chocolate cake too. One day, you will meet our good friend Doris. She makes the best and biggest chocolate cake ever!" laughed Christian. "Sometimes, she put lots of cherries on the top of the cake as well; I am sure the you will like Doris."

"Come on, let's go home now if we've all finished," said James, as soon as Christian has put down his knife and fork. "We need to collect Prince, and get Connor settled as it's getting late."

Still very concerned, but for the first time since they had left 'Hope Cottage', James felt a little happier that they had begun to make some progress in giving Connor some reassurance. He noticed that Christian had taken the boy's hand as they crossed the busy restaurant car park, and he was pleased to see that

Connor had happily accepted it, without reluctance, until they reached the car. On the long journey home, Connor fell asleep.

Chapter 5

It had been a long, and emotionally, exhausting day, and it was dark when James and Christian arrived home. Connor had slept all the way to Lavender Cottage. The small boy stepped into the cottage, wide eyed as the first impressions of his temporary home sunk in. After leaving James and Connor at the gate, Christian drove off to fetch Prince from Doris and George, whilst James set about making Connor feel at home. Fortunately, the spare room was already to receive the next visitor, with clean bedding and towels all in place.

"This is your room, Connor. The bathroom is next door, and you can leave your damp towels in there if you like. These drawers and the wardrobe are empty, so please use them when you empty your suitcase." James looked down at the small, brown, broken suitcase that he had dropped on the bed. It was very light, and emptying it wouldn't take very long.

Connor looked around the room in awe, gazing at the neatly prepared large double bed, colourful curtains and delicate cushions. He stared admiringly at the large photos and pictures on the walls, delicate ornaments on the dressing table and well-polished bedside cabinets.

"There's a lamp each side of the bed, if you want to read," smiled James, "which I suspect you do, since I heard you talking to Christian about all the books you've read. I hear you are a fan of 'The Lion, the Witch and the Wardrobe'. That's one of my favourites too. My class asks me to read it to them, or one of the sequels, each year; it's become a sort of school tradition, I think."

Connor's eyes lit up. "Is it, Mr Young? I'm really pleased you like it too. It's my favourite book of all time. I often wish I could travel through a wardrobe just like Peter, Susan, Edmund and Lucy."

"I sometimes wish that too," smiled James. "You can have a good look in our wardrobe if you like, Connor. I'm not sure if you will find an opening to Narnia, but if you are not down for breakfast tomorrow morning, I will know what has happened, and we'll come and look for you. I'm not sure what Prince would think of Aslan though!"

Connor gave a faint smile, nodded, and seemed to appreciate the idea.

"By the way, Connor, as you are going to be staying with us for a while, please call me James at home; you can call me Mr Young when we're in school."

Connor thought for a moment, "No, I will call you Mr Young if you don't mind, at least until I get to know you better. I hope you don't mind?

James paused for a moment. He was surprised because Connor had been calling Christian by his first name all day. "Not at all, Connor, call me whatever you like. Would you like to have a bath or shower tonight, or maybe tomorrow morning? Meanwhile, I'll go and get some food organised for when Christian arrives home with Prince."

"Maybe I'll do that in the morning. I can't wait to see Prince."

"Well you won't have to wait long, I can hear him coming in. Here he is! Hold on tight, he's a bit over enthusiastic at times.

A large, fluffy retriever bounded up the stairs, barking loudly as he smothered James with big licks and nearly pushed him to the ground. Christian leapt up the stairs behind him.

"Here he is Connor. This is Prince. He's just spent a lovely day with Doris and George. Doris is James' school secretary. You'll like her. She is our very best friend, isn't she James?"

"She certainly is," laughed James, as he was trying to rescue Connor from the over-enthusiastic dog. Connor was giggling as Prince pushed him to the ground, giving him big wet, friendly licks.

"Well, I think we can agree that Prince approves of you. I'm sure you two are going to be great friends," said Christian, hauling Connor up from the floor, with James holding firmly on to Prince's collar, to save Connor from yet more wet licks.

"He's a beautiful dog, but he's so big. Can we go for a walk with him now?"

"Let's do that tomorrow, as it's getting late; we need to eat now and then we can get you settled for the night. It's been a long day for all of us, hasn't it? Prince needs a rest too, as I think he will have spent the day walking with George and eating lots of food and treats from Doris. He will sleep for hours when he finally settles. When you're ready, come downstairs and we'll have some food," said James.

"I don't think I can eat any more after that lovely omelette, Mr Young, but I'll come down now with Prince.

Despite saying that he wasn't hungry, Connor did manage to eat the sandwich and soup that James had prepared for him, together with another glass of milk. After hugging Prince, and saying goodnight, Connor went up the stairs to his new bedroom, and the beginning of a new life in Lavender Cottage.

"Goodness knows what that poor lad must be thinking about after all that's happened," whispered Christian, as he got into bed beside James. "I'm so sorry to have started all this, James, whatever must you be thinking? This is a nightmare."

"Actually, in a strange way, I'm rather enjoying it," smiled James. "It's good to think about something other than the school extension. I like a new challenge, and Connor is certainly that. I feel so sorry for the boy, but we will do our best to help him. Prince certainly likes him, and he's very good at assessing character."

"That's true, but what do we do next? I've no need to tell you that we have put ourselves in a very difficult situation. To people who don't know us, it could be seen as child kidnapping. We have no documents or parents to contact to confirm any of this. Actually, I'm very worried, Jay."

"Yes, I am too. There are enough problems being a gay couple in a small community, but there's always that horrible view from some people that 'if they are gay they must be paedophiles'. We must be clever enough to help Connor, but also ensure that we protect ourselves."

"So, how do we do that, Jay? As a headteacher, you must be particularly careful, as this could prejudice your job."

"I was thinking about this all the way home. I do have a plan, and I'll start to put it into action tomorrow. Can you get some time off tomorrow and look after Connor? Maybe have a lazy day together, go for a walk with Prince and a little shopping in town? Please buy him a new toothbrush, as I don't think his teeth have been brushed in weeks."

"Good old, Jay," laughed Christian, gently rubbing his partner's back, "I knew you would be working on it. Actually, I've already called the office and asked for a week off, so that's no problem. Just tell me what you want me to do. I was wondering if we should buy Connor some new clothes? Those that he is wearing have a very strong smell, and his pullover, shirt and shorts are very grubby. His shorts have a tear in them too."

"Good idea, but be careful with that one, Chris. Yes, do buy a few essentials in town, but ask Connor first and get him involved in buying any clothes. He's been taken away from everything that he knows. I noticed that even in this warm weather, he is reluctant to take off his sweater, and when he does he kind of caresses it; a bit like a comfort blanket. I think it means something special to him. Offer to wash it, by all means, but don't throw it away.

Christian nodded. "Hmm, I hadn't thought of it like that. I can see that you did very well in your psychology course at college Mr Headmaster!"

"Don't call me that, you know I hate it!" hissed James. "Anyway, did I ever tell you that I got a first?"

Christian groaned as he hugged his partner, "You did actually, many times. Goodnight, Mr Headmaster…Ouch, that hurt!"

Chapter 6

The following morning, James got up early, prepared breakfast for Christian and Connor, as well as to feed Prince. A scruffy, unshaven Christian appeared at the kitchen door, closely followed by a smart looking Connor, who looked much fresher than he had done the day before. He had clearly had a shower, since his bright blonde hair was still wet and shining in the sunlight that shone through the kitchen window.

"Good morning you two, breakfast is ready, and Prince has already eaten and been outside for a run in the garden."

Connor was already on the floor stroking and playing with the happy dog, who was happily washing one of Connor's thin, spindly legs.

"Did you sleep alright, Connor?" asked James.

"I think it was best night ever," smiled Connor from somewhere in Prince's long, golden coat. "I've never been is such a big bed. I heard you get up, and then Christian came in and showed me how to use the shower. I didn't get on very well with that, so in the end I had a bath. I'm sorry, as I've spilled water all over the bathroom floor. I tried to mop it up with the towel, but it's still very wet."

"Don't worry, I know what you mean. Yes, that shower is a bit temperamental. We keep meaning to get it fixed. Do you want me to wash any of your clothes? If so, just put them in the basket over there, and I will put them in the washing machine after breakfast," said Christian, pouring himself a large bowl of cornflakes. "You come and sit over here, Connor. That is if Prince will let you."

"I'm off to the school this morning. It could be a long day, so you two enjoy yourselves and I'll cook something for us when I get back," said James, who grabbed his bag and headed towards the door.

"OK, have a good one, Jay. Don't worry about food. I'm taking Connor out to see Abbotsford later this morning. We'll get something special for our first proper home-cooked meal together. Connor tells me that he's a great cook, so I'm going to let him take charge!"

"I didn't say that," giggled Connor who was now seated in a chair that was far too low for him. "I just said that I was good at making sandwiches, but I am willing to learn."

"OK, it's a deal, young man. Now, don't you think you ought to have a cushion or two on your chair? Otherwise, I shall think I am having breakfast by myself."

James closed the door, and smiled as he saw the ease with which Christian was chatting with Connor. It was as if he was already the boy's big brother. James was pleased; he was a much more serious man by nature, and took time to get to know and trust people. Christian, on the other hand, was always everyone's friend from the moment that he met them, and no doubt a practice finely honed by selling properties, but it was a blessing in awkward circumstances, and particularly for the situation that they were in with Connor.

James drove the brief journey from Coombe to Prior's Hill, parked his car outside the parish church, and then walked across the narrow road to the school. James admired the beauty of the golden stone, which was now bathed in warm morning sunlight, that made up most of Prior's Hill properties. Apart from the church, school and Manor House, most of the dwellings were tied cottages belonging to the Peatwhistle Estate. As such, the buildings looked well maintained, albeit with all the cottage doors and window frames painted in exactly the same colour, which James didn't really approve of.

The socialist in James always made him irritated, when he remembered that nearly all the village belonged to the Peatwhistle family. He knew in his heart that it wasn't right, but he was also gradually coming to terms with its advantages. James was a firm believer in respect having to be earned and not automatically given through birth or financial assets. He knew from personal experience how much the Peatwhistles did for the village and the school. Sir Toby and Lady Lotitia Peatwhistle were always the first to help villagers in a crisis. When James first arrived at the school five years earlier, he found the school budget to be severely overspent, and he was unable to buy books and basic stationary for the new school year. James had complained to the school governors, and the following day, Sir Toby, who was the Chair of Governors, arrived at the school and handed James a personal cheque for a large sum with which he could fund these urgent needs for the new school year.

The Peatwhistle Estate employed many of the men and women who lived in the village, which brought both advantages and disadvantages to this small, close-knit community. The Peatwhistles were harsh, but fair employers; they did not offer generous wages, but James rarely heard a bad word or complaints being made against them. Cottages were well maintained, rents were low, a cash bonus, together with a large box of fruit and vegetables and a chicken were given to each employee at Christmas. James knew of families that had hit hard times, who discovered that their rent arrears had suddenly disappeared. At times of bereavement, the Peatwhistles were known to pay for the funeral. On one recent occasion they had paid for a sick child to be treated privately, as it was an urgent case that required specialist care. Although part of James heartily disapproved of privilege, he also reluctantly accepted that it usually worked in Prior's Hill, and no doubt due to the personality and consciences of the current incumbents.

James usually enjoyed walking though the old iron school gates, where there was a wonderful view of the beautiful golden stone building, accompanied by a large horse chestnut tree, under which he had spent many happy hours with his class on warm, sunny, summer days. It was under this tree that two villagers and good friends, Bert and Eddie, had built a wooden bench seat in memory of Tristan. The seat, now well-worn from use, still bore the brass plate and inscription. Bert and Eddie always ensured that the seat was well maintained, varnished each year and that the brass plate shone brightly. The inscription on the brass plate read 'In loving memory of Mr Tristan. A great friend of Prior's Hill School.' It was here also that James often sat to remember Tristan, and the happy times that they had shared. When sitting on this wooden bench, James would often lovingly rub the brass plate with his fingers, which made him feel close to Tristan once again.

Today, the playground looked different; the usually immaculately maintained playground was now covered with piles of sand, bags of cement, bricks, breeze blocks, concrete mixers and two large diggers. Even though the building work had started a few weeks earlier, the initial tidy piles of building materials had descended into chaos now that the school children were on holiday. James spotted the school caretaker, Cedric, wielding a large broom and attacking a small pile of sand.

"Good morning, Cedric. It's a mess isn't it?" shouted James, as he remembered that Cedric was hard of hearing and often forget to switch on his hearing aid. James, a generally quiet spoken man, was initially unaware of Cedric's hearing difficulties, and it was some weeks before Doris told James of his caretaker's problem.

"Good morning, Mr Young. Yes, it is. Actually, I'm very annoyed with what they are doing. It doesn't have to be like this."

"Don't you bother cleaning it up for them, Cedric. That's their job and I'll be telling them so shortly. You have quite enough to do indoors."

"Right you are, Sir, I'll leave this and get back to my floors then. I'm sanding and polishing this week. I've got a new sealant from County Hall to try as well. They'll really shine up by the time I've finished."

James nodded, "I know that, Cedric. You always make such a good job of the floors, and visitors often comment how good they look."

"It's just a pity that the kids have to walk on them," commented Cedric, nodding thoughtfully.

James didn't know whether Cedric was being serious, but laughed anyway. "Right, I'm off to tell those builders what I think of them. I'll be in school for a few hours, as I've got a few phone calls to make, but I'll see you before I go. Fancy a coffee? I'm just about to make one for myself."

"Right you are, Sir. Yes, I'd love a coffee if you're making one. I'll be around until about four today," said Cedric, feeling just a little sorry for the builder who would shortly be at the receiving end of James' wrath. James was a fair man, in Cedric's opinion, but "He don't suffer fools," was the usual comment made to his wife. "No. James don't suffer fools at all."

Cedric still remembered the time when the building work began on an earlier school extension and a few layers of breeze blocks had been put in place. James had stood watching for a few moments, before addressing the offending builder, telling him that they were not level, and did he need to borrow a spirit level? Apparently, the builder had turned very red and disputed James' assessment of his work. James reappeared a few minutes later with a spirit level and triumphantly proved to the builder that he, James, was correct and that the builder should be more careful as he didn't want an extension leaning to one side. The builder, again red faced, apologised and started the job from the beginning. Cedric often told the story, suitably enhanced over a pint in his local, complete with the accompanying foul language that the builder had offered when James was no longer in sight.

Yes, James was a man of detail, and when it came to his school and the children that he cared for; he took no prisoners. Today though, unusually, James didn't cast his usual critical eye on the progress of the building work, but instead he headed indoors and upstairs to his office.

James had decided and discussed with Christian the night before that he needed to make three important phone calls. The first call would be to Sarah Tibbles, the school's social worker. James had known Miss Tibbles since he had first arrived at the school. She was a wearisome soul, no doubt always having a heavy and impossible case load, and who enjoyed telling the world how badly she was treated. Despite this, she had helped James on several occasions, and he was always ready to be generous towards those who helped his children and the school. Miss Tibbles was also grossly overweight, as well as being a keen naturist. James often wondered what the other group members thought of her on their many rambles together.

"Good morning, James. I thought you would be on holiday and not working. I'm very busy today, I've got so many people to see. Is it really urgent?"

"It really is urgent, Sarah," replied James. "As I'm sure you know, I wouldn't ask if it wasn't urgent, but I have a serious and pressing personal problem. I am sure that you can help me, as you have done in the past. You always get to the heart of the problem and know what to do."

A spot of flattery always worked well with Miss Tibbles, and James always knew just when to apply it.

"Alright, I'll try to be there later this morning. How about at eleven?"

"Perfect, thank you so much. I look forward to seeing you then," said James, putting the phone down and making a careful note in his diary.

The second phone call was to PC Trickle. Nick Trickle was a young police officer whom James had got to know very well. His two young daughters now attended the school, and James had made a point of encouraging PC Trickle to become a school governor. He had since been elected as a parent governor, and James had already found this enthusiastic police officer invaluable. James and Nick had also become good friends and they would occasionally meet for a drink in the village pub. James decided to call Nick at home, instead of the police station.

Mary Trickle, Nick's wife, answered the call, sounding flustered. "Hello, Mr Young. No, I'm sorry, Nick is at the station right now. I'll get him to give you a call if you like. Is it urgent?"

"Yes, Mary, it is, I'm afraid. That would be good if you could get him to call me. I'm in school right now and I'll wait for his call."

The third phone call was to Lotitia Peatwhistle, Lady of the Manor, and surprisingly, one of James' and Christian's closest friends. They had shared some very serious times together in the past, but in more recent times enjoyed, tolerated and later revelled in each other's company. Lotitia Peatwhistle had a fondness for gin, was often late arising and even later turning in. She was clearly a woman who had enjoyed life to the full when she was younger, but now busied herself with the duties of the Lord of the Manor's wife. She enjoyed dominating events, loved gossip, endured endless cutting of ribbons at charity events, but most of all enjoyed riotous get-togethers with her two gay friends, James and Christian.

It was a strange relationship indeed, and in the early days, James and Lotitia had come to many verbal blows around the subjects of fox hunting, which James detested and Lady Lotitia regularly indulged, the Conservative Party, the evils of feudal villages and the irrelevance of the House of Lords. Christian had often sat in embarrassed silence as James expounded his views, whilst Lotitia enjoyed batting off the insults rather like an endless volley of tennis balls being hit at her. It became even more lively as the gin flowed and the early evening turned into early morning. The verbal spats always ended in good humour, and James always admired Lotitia's great skill in always triumphantly declaring that she was right, whatever the subject and outcome of their debates. James and Lotitia also shared horrendous events that had formed the basis of much of their relationship. It was a sacred bond of trust and mutual affection that could not be broken.

"Humph, I guess you would like to see the Manor House turned into flats for the unwashed masses, James, what? That's what would really suit you. Have you thought who would employ all the villagers if we weren't here, what?"

As James got to know the Peatwhistles better, as well as growing older and a little wiser with the experience and realities of life, he gradually came to terms that life in the village was a fine balance and that the Peatwhistles were more of a force for good than bad. It was by no means perfect, but it served a purpose. He shuddered to think what life would be like in other communities if the local aristocracy were not so thoughtful and benevolent. Over the years, James had come to appreciate Lady Lotitia's sense of humour and they would both delight in wickedly teasing each other.

"Hello, Lotitia, It's James. Are you up yet?"

"Of course I am, young man. What do you think I do all day? I've been up for at least five minutes. I've got a dinner party to plan, a new dress to be fitted and a new brand of gin to try. What can I do for you?"

"May I call to see you later? I need to talk to you about something quite serious."

"I don't like the sound of that, what! I hope you are not telling me that you are leaving us. I really cannot allow that. Yes, of course, I'm in all day, just call when you can. Bring that lovely boy with you too, what!"

James nearly asked which "lovely boy" she was referring to. It could be Christian, of whom she was very fond, Prince, whom Lotitia adored, or maybe she already knew about Connor. James' heart sank when he thought this, because Lotitia always had to be the first to know about everything happening in 'her' village.

"No, it'll just be me. You'll understand when I see you."

"I hope you're not going to tell me that you two have split up!"

"No, it's nothing like that. Christian is well and happy, and Prince is well too, if a little over fed. I am wondering why that is, Lotitia?"

"You blaming me? Stuff and nonsense, what?" exclaimed Lotitia. "See you later, James."

There was a click as Lotitia put the phone down.

The school phone rang. It was Nick Trickle. "Hello James, Mary tells me that you want to speak to see me."

"Hello, Nick, thank you for getting back to me. I need to speak with you about something that has cropped up. Would you be able to come over to the school?"

"Is there a problem at the school, James? I've just got to finish filing a report and then I'll be over to see you."

"No, it's a personal matter, Nick. You may be able to help."

"I'll do what I can, James, you know that. See you shortly."

James heaved a sigh of relief as he put the phone down. He was indeed fortunate to be surrounded by such good friends and people who he knew would try to help. James wandered into the small kitchen, filled and switched on the kettle and made himself a mug of coffee for both himself and Cedric. He also opened a fresh packet of chocolate biscuits, which was one of his weaknesses that he knew Cedric shared.

Later that morning, Sarah Tibbles, the school's social worker, arrived at the school. James was pleased to see her and greeted her with a kiss and offered her a cup of coffee, but not a biscuit, since he considered that Sarah could do with a going on a very strict diet.

"No thank you, James. In my job, I'm always being offered coffee. Sometimes I go home as high as a kite and cannot sleep," said Sarah, accompanied by a ripple of nervous laughter.

"I know what you mean," agreed James. "I drink far too much coffee here too. I don't really know why, as I never really enjoy it or have time to finish it. It does seem to keep me going on some of those difficult days though.

Sarah Tibbles listened attentively to what James began to say. Just as James had started his story, there was another knock on the door; it was PC Nick Trickle.

"Come in, Nick. Thank you for coming over at short notice. You know Sarah, of course."

Sarah smiled and nodded at PC Trickle, who shook her hand and sat down.

"The extension seems to be progressing nicely, James. When will it be finished?"

"It's moving on nicely now," agreed James, "but it has been a battle. The building work is almost finished, thank goodness. The carpenters, plasters and fitters are already making good progress inside. Another couple of weeks and I hope the decorators will be in and it will be ready for use. We can then start letting the children use it when they return. We are so dreadfully cramped at the moment. Those temporary classrooms can then be taken away, thank goodness."

"My girls can't wait," said PC Trickle, "I guess you will have some form of grand opening; ribbon cutting, sandwiches, wine and all that?"

James noticed that Sarah seemed to perk up considerably at this suggestion.

"That's a difficult one," grinned James. "Lady Lotitia seem to think that she will be cutting the ribbon, but the Diocese tells me that Bishop Colin has it in his diary and is planning to open it. Goodness knows how Lady Lotitia will take the news. After all, it was Sir Toby, as well as Bishop Colin that managed to get us the new building."

Sarah giggled, "That is a difficult one, James. Rather you than me; she is such a formidable lady. Anyway, we had better get on and hear what you have to say, since I have to shoot off to another meeting soon."

James began his story again, and both Sarah Tibbles and PC Trickle listened attentively to what he had to say.

Sarah sighed, "Well you have certainly landed yourself with a difficult one this time, James. You do realise that you and Mr Trill could be seen as kidnappers and prosecuted? My best advice is to get the boy into the hands of the Cornwall local authority right away. They should be able to place him in a care home, or foster parents if any are available at short notice, and there is always a shortage. Whatever you do, the boy cannot stay with you."

"Do you have any paperwork, or letter of agreement from the grandmother, James?" asked PC Trickle, opening his notebook.

"Nothing," said James. "It sounds foolish now, but the old lady said she was very ill; dying, in fact. Connor was in the room, and it just seemed the right thing to do under the distressing circumstances that we found ourselves in. To be honest, we were pleased to get away. The whole situation was so weird."

"It doesn't help that you are a same-sex couple looking after a child," began Sarah. "People talk and come to conclusions. This could quickly get out of hand and be a threat to your job, James. I'm sure you know that?"

"This is precisely why I have asked you both here today, to tell you what has happened and ask for your advice; I want this to be recorded too, just in case. It goes without saying that you are both welcome to visit our home at any time to check us out, as well as Connor. You have both been to our home many times anyway, and already know Christian.

"We do indeed, James, and frankly I can think of no better people to look after a vulnerable child," said PC Trickle. "However, Sarah is right. We must be careful, both for the boy's sake and for yourselves. I will make some enquiries with my colleagues in Bodmin, and try to find where the grandmother is, and hopefully get her written permission for you to take temporary care of the boy."

Sarah nodded. "I'll check with my colleagues in Bodmin too, as well as the schools there, and see what I can find out. Meanwhile, I suggest that you take the boy to see a doctor for a thorough check up. Get a written report; it may come in useful later, James. I cannot stress this enough."

James nodded, "Good advice, I will do as you say. Just one more thing, whilst I was waiting for you both this morning, I checked out all the hospitals in Bodmin, and indeed Cornwall. I cannot find a St Agnes Hospital anywhere in the county."

PC Trickle nodded, "Well, that was going to be one line of my enquiries. I guess it could be a private facility, a hospice, or for those with psychiatric problems. I'll make that a priority."

"Be very careful, James. I know from experience that good deeds such as this can easily blow up in your face," warned Sarah, as she walked out of the door.

Chapter 7

The next two weeks passed by quickly, and both James and Christian agreed that they were some of the happiest that they had shared together. Christian had taken some time off work, and James, for once, only disappeared briefly each morning to check upon developments with the school building, before returning home to Christian, Connor and Prince. James had put Cedric 'in charge' and asked him to call James at once if there was a problem he could not handle. Cedric appeared to be delighted with the additional responsibility and trust placed in him, and assured James that he would do his best.

James, Christian, Connor and Prince spent the next two weeks on long walks, picnics, teaching Connor to swim, as well as meeting with Doris and George and, of course, Lady Lotitia.

It soon became clear, that Connor had rarely seen the sea, let alone been paddling or swimming. On one glorious summer day they headed to their local beach.

"I'm going in for a swim, Connor. It looks glorious out there. You coming in with me?" asked Christian, enthusiastically.

Conor looked embarrassed and shook his head. "No thank you, Christian. I don't really feel like it. I'll watch you from here."

James, Connor and Prince lay on the old car rug that Christian had thrown on the sand for them, and watched Christian rip off his clothes and head for the sea. James admired his partner's stocky, muscly, tanned body and the way that he attacked the waves in his strong, determined swimming style.

"Christian is a very good swimmer," commented Connor. "I don't think I've been to the seaside before. There are a lot of people here."

"You've never been to the seaside?" asked James, incredulously. "You've never sat on the beach or paddled in the water?"

Connor shook his head. "I've seen the sea, of course, Mr Young, but I've never sat by it or been in the water. It's lovely isn't it?"

James nodded, and realised once again, how much this young boy had missed in his few years of life. He and Christian had already learned to be very careful in their questioning, and didn't ask Connor too many questions at any one time. Although the boy was much more communicative than when they had first met, asking more than a few questions would result in Connor looking flushed and close to tears. He would then clam up and not speak again for some time, as if deep in thought and wondering what to say.

"Can you swim, Connor? I was wondering if you have ever been swimming in a pool, and not the sea."

Connor shook his head, and paused for a moment watching Christian fooling around with Prince on the water's edge. "I would like to. I could then go in the water with Prince, couldn't I?"

James laughed, "Yes, Prince would love that. Well, I'll teach you, if you like. Maybe not in the school swimming pool, as we are having a few problems with it at the moment. We could ask Lady Lotitia if we could use her pool, and I could teach you to swim there."

Connor laughed, and his beaming smile delighted James. It was so rare to see, but so welcome when it came, as the young boy rarely showed any emotion of delight.

"I'd love that Mr Young. I like Lady Lotitia; she's a little weird, but in a nice way. She let me borrow some of her books when we went to see her the other day."

"I know what you mean, Connor. She is a very nice lady, and she certainly has taken to you. Yes, I notice that you came home with quite a collection. Did I see Gulliver's Travels, Robinson Crusoe and Alice in Wonderland in your bag?"

"Yes, and Nicholas Nickleby, Oliver Twist and David Copperfield. I love books by Charles Dickens, but they make me sad sometimes."

"They are amazing stories, but why do they make you sad, Connor?"

"Well, they are all about boys that are not very well treated. I don't want to go to a school like Dotheboys Hall. I'm worried that if Gran doesn't come home, and I cannot stay with you and Christian, they will put me in a school like that."

James put an arm around the small boy. "Listen to me, young man. Whatever happens, you are not going to a place like that. Christian and I will never let that happen to you. If anything happens to your Gran, we would want you to stay with us and we will do anything that we can to make that happen."

Later that night, Christian commented that he could not believe the transformation in James' attitude. He seemed so relaxed and the excessive tiredness had all but disappeared.

"Well, to be honest, I'm rather enjoying being a Dad to Connor," confided James to Christian one night. "The boy needs us, and I am enjoying being a family. For once, work is not a priority for me."

Christian nodded, "I agree, James. I love you and always enjoy our times together, but Connor seems to have added something very special to our relationship."

"I'm dreading when he has to go back to Cornwall. It's been more than two weeks now, and I know I should contact social services again, but I'm afraid to do so. I know what it will mean. Connor seems so happy with us; as for Prince…"

Christian laughed, "I think we have lost our dog. He adores Connor. Have you noticed the way that he looks at him, and follows him wherever he goes?"

"I have, and don't think I haven't noticed that he now sleeps on Connor's bed every night: Actually, it's rather nice to be able to turn in bed without Prince being in the way. Connor loves him too."

"Christian, if there was a way, would you be happy for Connor to live with us permanently?" asked James hesitantly.

"Of course. Need you ask me that? I adore the boy, and I've been thinking exactly the same thing, but I can't see how that can ever be possible.

As agreed with Miss Tibbles, James made an appointment for Connor to see their Doctor, Dr Emerson, who had a surgery in Abbotsford. He told the doctor a little about the circumstances that they were in, but not the detail. As far as Dr Emerson was concerned, they were looking after Connor temporarily for a sick relative, but were concerned about the boy's weight.

"Well, Mr Young," began Dr Emerson, "Connor appears to be in generally good health, but he is grossly underweight for his age, and under nourished. You are right to be concerned, because in a case such as this, it can lead to other issues later in life. The boy needs a good healthy diet, lots of good food, plenty of milk, fresh air and some sunshine on his body. He seems to be generally fit, and has good muscle strength, but I see him as a six-year-old and not a nine-year-old boy. However, what an intelligent and articulate boy he seems to be for his age! I'll write all this up for you and send you the report. Would you like me to send a copy to social services as well?"

Dr Emerson peered over his half-moon glasses, smiling questioningly at James.

"Don't worry," said Dr Emerson before James could reply, "I have had enough experiences in this job to know that you are not telling me everything. I think I know the reasons why, and you have my full support. Prior's Hill is a small community and I hear things."

"I'm sorry, Dr Emerson. We are in a difficult situation through no fault of our own. Yes, do please send a copy of the report to Miss Tibbles."

Chapter 8

The doorbell rang; it was Doris carrying a large plastic box. Prince barked with enthusiasm and bounded towards the tiny woman, and almost knocked her to the ground as she entered Lavender Cottage.

"I know, I know, I've got a treat for you as well, Prince. Hello again, Connor, are you having a good time with James and Christian? I can see that Prince adores you."

"Good morning, Mrs Cole. It is so lovely to see you again. Yes, I love Prince too, he's a wonderful dog. He's my friend now. Have you brought a chocolate cake for us? I think I can see it through the plastic lid."

"Yes, I made this one just for you, Connor. I also know you like cherries, so I've put a lot of large, juicy ones on the top. You may wish to share it with James and Christian?"

Connor gave one of his sparkling laughs, "Yes, of course I will, Mrs Cole. It won't last long though. Prince likes it too!"

"Heavens! I hope you are not giving that dog cake as well! He is quite plump enough already, Connor."

"Only a little piece. He is having lots of walks, and Christian takes him swimming, so I guess he will be alright with all that exercise."

"OK, I'll let you off with that one, Connor. Where are James and Christian?"

"We're here," came a voice that Doris recognised as Christian's. "We're in the living room."

Connor led Doris into the living room. On the floor were two men playing with a small train set.

"What are you boys doing?" laughed Doris, looking amazed, since she could never imagine James playing with toy trains.

"It's Christian's old train set. It's been stored in the loft since we came here, and we thought we'd get it down and let Connor play with it."

"Have you played with it yet, Connor?" laughed Doris, winking at Connor who was giggling beside her.

"Er, not yet, but I hope to. Maybe when Christian and Mr Young have finished playing with it. It looks like a lot of fun."

The next few days were very happy ones, with James and Christian reliving their inner childhood, and being caring, supportive parents, and a small boy who began to experience what it was truly like to be happy with the love and support of a family that truly cared for him.

The telephone rang. James and Christian had been waiting for a phone call for several days, and James was sure that this was the call that they had been waiting for. He just knew it would be bad news and that their few weeks of happiness would shortly be coming to an end.

"Good morning, James," came Sarah's voice, "I'm sorry I've not been able to get back to you before, but I've just heard from Cornwall. To cut a long story short, they have tried to find Mrs Viers, and they cannot track her down to any hospital in the area. They say that they have been in contact with some of the local schools and there is no Connor Viers registered with any of them."

"I think that's very doubtful, Sarah. As you know, schools are currently closed for the holidays. I doubt social services would be able to get that kind of information from any of them. I have tried myself, but everyone is on holiday."

"Maybe they just checked with County Hall for registrations then, James. One interesting thing was that I heard from the attendance officer for that area, and he said that they had received a report from a local farmer that there was a small, deaf boy living close to the farm who never seemed to go to school. He was left on his own quite a lot, always seemed hungry, and the farmer and his wife were worried about him."

"That's more like it, Sarah. Have they been to check it out?"

"The attendance officer tried to visit several weeks ago, but no one answered the door, and he assumed that nobody was at home."

"Did he follow it up?" demanded James.

"Sadly, no. That seemed to be the end of the matter until I received the call today. I had already expressed surprise that no one had checked upon a child at risk since that first visit, and so he visited again yesterday."

Sarah paused.

"and …?" interrupted James, desperate to move on with the story. He could almost guess the next part.

"When he visited again, the cottage was empty. He looked through the windows, but there was no furniture, no beds and no personal effects. Nothing. He checked with the farmer who told him that the old lady had moved out several weeks ago, but he didn't know where she had gone. Apparently, she told him to empty the cottage and to get rid of everything, as she would not be returning, because she was very ill. The rent was fully paid up to date though. The farmer had the cottage cleared of furniture, and the few items were stored in one of his barns until he could decide what to do with them. The cottage will now be renovated and rented out as a holiday cottage. I also checked this with PC Trickle, and he tells me that his opposite number in Bodmin has just discovered the same thing. There is simply no evidence of Mrs Viers currently living in the cottage, no idea where she has gone, and no evidence of any other relatives. Other than what the farmer has said, it is as if the woman has never existed."

"So, what happens to Connor now?" asked James.

"The Cornwall office tells me that the boy must be returned to their care, since they can trace no living relatives. They plan to either collect Connor from you as soon as a care place has been found, or ask me to take him to Bodmin for them. The details of the transfer have still to be worked out."

"I see, it all seems so cold. This is a small, frightened little boy that we are talking about," replied James, anxious not to let his true feelings be known. "I understand the situation though. Please, keep me in touch, and let me know when you have more information. Thank you for getting back to me. By the way, did you say that the farmer thought he was deaf?"

"Yes, that's what they told me, but that's a bit odd in itself, because Connor doesn't have a hearing problem, does he? I'm sorry, James. I gather that you have both become very fond of the boy, but you know that it's impossible for you to adopt or even foster him on a permanent basis, even though you would be ideal in so many ways."

"Thank you, Sarah," said James, choking back tears. He would now have to break the news to Christian and, worse still, to Connor.

Chapter 9

Christian sat in silence in the kitchen, thinking about the last few weeks and dreading what was likely to happen next. Prince sat with James, occasionally licking his hand in reassurance. James and Connor were playing with the old train set that they had recently set up, and Connor was talking enthusiastically to James about his ideas for improvements to the general layout.

"I think we should have a bridge over there, because at the moment, passengers have to cross that field to change platforms. On a wet day, it would get very muddy. I also think that signal box is in the wrong place. What do you think, Mr Young?"

"Well spotted, you are right, Connor," responded James, although he couldn't muster much enthusiasm, as he was thinking about how and when they would break the recent news to Connor.

The telephone rang again. "Can you get that please, James?" yelled Christian from the kitchen, "I'm getting lunch."

"James, this is me again," announced Doris. It often irritated the sometimes-pedantic James when Doris announced herself in this manner on the telephone. After all, it could be anyone, except it couldn't be really, since Doris had such a distinctive voice.

"James, I need to see you, right away; it's urgent. Can you come over now?"

"Of course, I can, if it's that urgent, Doris. I'll come right away."

"James?"

"Yes Doris?"

"Please don't bring Connor."

After making very brief excuses about Doris having a crisis to Christian and Connor, James ran out of the cottage, and then had to run back to the cottage again to collect the car keys.

"I forgot the Spitfire keys. Don't wait for me, I may be some time. Save me some lunch please, Connor, don't eat it all. It already smells delicious."

James breathlessly ran back to the Spitfire, started it up and headed down the road to see Doris. It was only a ten-minute journey, but James always enjoyed the excuse to drive the car.

When he arrived at Doris and George's smart bungalow, Doris was already waiting at the door to greet him.

"James, I've discovered something very important about Connor... You know I like word games?"

James nodded, as he remembered Doris sitting under the old horse chestnut tree, on Tristan's bench. She could usually be found completing crossword puzzles or Sudoku in the school playground at the end of the day on the rare occasions when she had finished her work.

"I was making up record cards for the new intake of children. I assumed Connor would be amongst them, so I was making up a card for him too. As I was writing his name, it suddenly occurred to me that something was not right."

"What do you mean?" asked James, beginning to feel even more anxious than when he arrived.

"Look at the name, Mrs Viers. Look M-R-S-V-I-E-R-S … it's almost a perfect anagram for …

"Sam Rivers!" yelled James, going pale and now sitting on the kitchen stool. "Oh no, it can't be, it's him again, Doris. I know it is!"

"Don't you two be so hasty, "counselled George, as he entered the kitchen. George, who was as equally challenged in height as his wife, was a cautious, fun loving man, who loved nothing more than to tease his often-serious wife. "It's probably nothing more than coincidence. Anyway, it's not a perfect anagram is it? It could mean something or nothing. Do more research and don't jump to conclusions is my best advice. Anyway, as you know, James, Doris loves a good drama, don't you my dear?"

Doris threw a tea towel at her grinning husband. "It's nothing to joke about, so please don't be so flippant. This is serious, and James and Christian are worried sick about the boy. I am too."

"I'm sorry," apologised George, "I was just trying to lighten the situation."

"Well don't," snapped Doris.

"Do you remember when we were all at Lotitia's last week, and you were teaching Connor to swim in her pool. I was watching Connor then, and it was his blonde hair that suddenly reminded me of Sam Rivers. It flashed through my mind briefly, but then I realised that Connor hasn't the same physique and, apart from his hair, is nothing like Sam, but …"

"So, Sam Rivers could be Connor's father…" began James, thoughtfully. "I've fallen for his tricks yet again. I'm so thick sometimes, I just cannot see through the obvious. Anyway, it could be that he takes after his mother, whoever that is?"

"Never mind, son," said George, putting his hand on James' shoulder. "You are not thick, by any means. You're simply too trusting, and you believe what you see and what people tell you. It's a good quality and nothing to be ashamed of. It's those people who try to deceive you with secrets and lies who should be ashamed of themselves."

"Well, that's the most sensible thing that you've said all day, George," agreed Doris.

James returned to Lavender Cottage, both angry and upset. Christian could see that something was wrong, as soon as he entered the doorway.

"Is everything alright with Doris? I was worried as you left so quickly."

"She's fine, but we need to talk, and I think we need to do it now!" thundered James, angrily.

Christian looked concerned. He had rarely seen James lose his temper, but when he did, all reason seemed to disappear. Christian had learned to be careful during these moments.

"Right, lunch is on hold. Connor is in the living room. Do you want do it here or the living room?"

"Let's go into the living room," said James, quickly calming down. "I need to talk to you both. It's serious stuff."

"Connor, I've just been to see Doris," said James, speaking slowly and gently. "She told me something that I am very worried about, and it's about you."

"Yes, Mr Young?" questioned Connor sitting on the rug next to Prince, who was looking adoringly at him and giving him a series of wet licks. Connor's bright, piercing blue eyes were focussed upon James and what he had to say.

"Is Sam Rivers your father?" blurted out James. Christian's jaw dropped open in amazement, and the small boy paused briefly, and took a deep breath.

"Yes, Mr Young, he is."

"The grandmother that we met when we came to see you. Was that really your Dad dressed up and pretending to be an old lady?" James asked, but his voice became sharper with anger.

Connor nodded, his face turned bright red as he began to cry. "I'm sorry, I'm so sorry. Please don't hate me, please don't hate me, Mr Young!" he sobbed.

Christian leapt off his seat and sat on the floor beside Connor, gently putting his arm around him and comforting the small boy.

"We could never hate you, Connor," said James quietly, "but we just need to know the truth. It's very serious, because today I had a call from social services telling me that they want to collect you and take you back to Cornwall. We don't want that to happen, we want to help you, but you must help us to do that. Do you understand what I'm saying, Connor?"

The tear-stained boy nodded miserably. "I don't want to go back. I want to stay here with you, Christian and Prince. Please don't send me back," he sobbed.

There was a pause as James reflected upon what he should say and do next. Christian's arm continued to reassure Connor, whilst Prince continued to give him comforting wet licks.

Suddenly, Connor stood up, left the room and ran up the stairs. A few seconds later, he returned with a thick, white envelope that he thrust into James' hand.

He returned to the rug and continued stroking Prince, and waited for a reaction.

James stared at the white envelope with the words 'To Mr James Young' written in bold handwriting and in black ink across its centre. The word 'PRIVATE' was written in capital letters across the top left-hand side, and underlined twice. James immediately recognised the handwriting and very carefully opened the thick envelope. He briefly glanced at the signature at the bottom and left the room.

Chapter 10

James sat on the bed, reading the long, handwritten letter. It was painstakingly written, and James immediately recognised the distinctive, scrawled handwriting that he had last read three years earlier, which was Sam's attempt to impersonate Tristan's handwriting. He gave a deep sigh as he read the words before him:

Dear James,

First of all, I'm sorry for what I have put you through in the last few years. Thank you also for looking after my son, Connor. If you are reading this letter, something has gone wrong and Connor has given you this letter, as I asked him to.

The truth is, I guess I was always very jealous of your relationship with Tristan. I have loved you since the first time that we met, but it was not to be. Instead of moving on, I stalked you with bad intentions and cunning. You are a good man and you were easy to trick and deceive; I am so sorry for my appalling behaviour.

I have had therapy, and I believe that I am a much better person, but things are now going badly wrong for me. Connor's mother died when he was a baby and Rita's mother looked after him for me until two years ago. Until that time, I had hardly any contact with him and didn't know the boy. Two years ago, Rita's mother also died and I suddenly had to look after Connor myself. I didn't really know how, but we managed. I had recently been discharged from a psychiatric hospital, and I felt that I could cope better with life and provide some kind of home for Connor. I became very fond of the boy during that period.

To ensure Connor's future, I had to get some money very quickly. You see, I am now HIV positive, and I know that I have a limited time left. I worked in England, as well as Spain, for many weeks, and earned quite a lot of money. As usual, I got mixed up with some bad people, and we had to keep moving to make sure that they and the police did not find me. As you know, hiding from people is something that I am very good at, but it is Connor who has suffered in the process of keeping my secret. At the moment, I am mostly well, but I have some very bad days.

This bring me to you, James. I have watched and admired you over the years, and I know that you always do the best that you can for the children at your school. As you know, my real mother hates me, and I have no relatives who want anything to do with me, or who I can ask to care for Connor when I'm gone. I beg that you and Christian take care of Connor for me. As I am sure that you know already, Connor is a clever boy, although I say so myself.

I know that I am asking a lot of you both, and you owe me no favours, but you are the only ones that I trust will love and look after my son, as I wish I could. I have only known Connor for a short time, but I love him very much and want the best for him. Please help me to do this.

If I am well enough, I plan to return to Spain to collect some bad debts and to put right some of the wrongs that I have caused. I doubt that you will ever hear from me again. When the time comes, please speak to Mr Carter at Carter and Miller in Abbotsford. Jim Carter will know what to do next.

Please look after Connor, as the son that you never had.

With my love and best wishes to you, Christian and Connor.

Sam

Christian's head appeared around the door, "Are you OK, Jay? Do you want to be alone or can I come in?"

"Of course you can, Chris. Take a look at this letter and let me know what you think? I'd better go now and see Connor. He'll be wondering what's going on."

Christian nodded, looking very serious, and took the letter from James. "Connor's still very upset, but Prince is looking after him. Seems that Sam is up to his old tricks again. You must be very careful not to fall into one of his traps. He is a nasty, devious piece of work, and I thought we had seen the last of him."

James nodded and left the room thoughtfully.

When James arrived back in the living room, he sat down on the sofa, and asked Connor to join him.

"Look, Connor, whatever happens, Christian and I will do the very best we can for you. To help us to do that you must tell us everything you know. You're a sensible boy, so we will also tell you exactly what's going on too. No more secrets and no more lies, agreed?"

Connor nodded, and wiped away his tears. "Is my Dad dead, Mr Young? He told me he wasn't very well, and sometimes he was quite sick. Other times, he was like he always is."

James listened, not wanting to upset the boy again, but determined that there would be no more secrets; no more lies. "I think your Dad is alive, but I don't know. It's important that we find out where he is, and try to help him. Do you know where he is?"

"Spain," said Connor, without any hesitation. He always goes there in the summer because of the tourists; they tip him well. He goes to a place called Benidorm."

"Good, I know Benidorm," nodded James. "Do you know what he's doing there?"

Connor thought for a moment. "He usually works in a circus as an acrobat or clown, I think, but this year he is working at a Cowboy place. He plays Cowboys and Indians. He told me that he likes it there."

James looked puzzled and shook his head. "Is it a bar, or maybe a theatre?"

"I don't know much more, Mr James. He told me that he has to dress up as a cowboy and someone tries to shoot him. He also has to go into a snake pit with real snakes," Connor shuddered, "I didn't like the sound of that."

"Neither do I, Connor," replied James, wincing. He didn't care for snakes either.

Christian returned quietly to the living room, looking very serious, and sat in the seat opposite James and Connor. Prince leapt on to the sofa, and sat beside James and Connor.

"I've told Connor that there will be no more secrets in this house," began James. "We will tell him everything that's going on, and he will tell us all that he knows to help us find his Dad."

"Good plan," agreed Christian. "So, what do we do next?"

"Well, I've told Connor that we should find his Dad and try to help him. Sam wants us to look after Connor, but we must get his written agreement first."

Connor's eyes lit up. "You mean I can stay here with you, Christian and Prince?"

James hesitated, but after all, he had agreed to be honest with the boy. "These things are not easy, Connor. As you know Christian and I are two men living together. People like us are not allowed to adopt children in this country. In other countries, same-sex couples can, but not in England just yet. Maybe one day we will too."

Connor's face fell. "I know lots of gay people. My Dad is gay sometimes, and he has lots of boyfriends; some I like, others I don't. I don't understand why I cannot stay with you, if that's what my Dad wants."

"We'll see what we can do. Let's stay positive and try not to worry too much about it now. First, we must find your Dad and get his agreement that he wants us to help him."

"What about this Mr Carter," interrupted Christian. "I guess he's a solicitor? Do you think you should speak with him first?"

"Yes, I think we must do that right away and before we do anything else. I'll call him now. This has all been very serious, hasn't it? Look, Connor, why don't you and Christian take Prince for a run in the woods, whilst I phone Mr Carter?"

When James and Christian were on their own again that night, James retold what Mr Carter had said to him.

"I know Jim Carter. I think his grandson was at the school for a short time before the family moved away. He seems to be a good man, but was very cautious in what he told me. Basically, he said he could tell me nothing until I gave him the right papers and only then could he open Sam's file and answer my questions."

"Papers, what papers?" asked Christian.

"I don't really know and he wouldn't be drawn on that. I asked if he meant a death certificate, or something saying that Sam was incapacitated, but he wouldn't answer. I also asked him if he knew where Sam was, and he said he couldn't answer that either.

"In other words, not at all helpful. For Christ's sake, does he not know or care that we have a small boy at risk here? Did he mention Connor at all?" asked Christian angrily.

"I mentioned Connor and the problem that we now have, but he ignored my questions. He was polite, but non-committal."

"Bloody solicitors," muttered Christian.

"I think I have no alternative but to go to Spain as soon as I can," began James. "I can maybe get a flight out there tomorrow. I vaguely remember Benidorm but ..."

"You can't possibly go there on your own!" interrupted Christian. "This may be yet another one of Sam's cruel, pointless tricks. You know what he's like, this could be very dangerous for you. Let me come with you."

James hugged Christian, "I know you care about me, but I have to do this on my own. Anyway, who would look after Connor and Prince?"

"I've already thought about that. Doris and George would love to have them stay with them. Doris adores Connor, and I think it's mutual. As for Prince, there are so many folk in the village offering to look after him when we are away, I wouldn't know where to start!"

"That's not really fair on Connor, Chris. He's only just started getting used to us. I would worry all the time about him. No, please stay with him and I'll go alone. I promise I'll be careful. I'll phone you every night, I promise."

Christian always knew when James had made his mind up, and decided not to argue anymore.

"Alright, alright. I'll stay here, but be warned that if I don't hear from you each evening, Jay, I'll be on the next flight out to find you!"

Chapter 11

It was an early morning flight, and Christian had booked a taxi to take James to the airport. James kissed the still sleeping Christian goodbye, and crept downstairs quietly so as not to wake Connor and Prince. Sadly, it was too late, since Prince and Connor were already sitting in the kitchen waiting expectantly for him.

"Hello you two. Why are you up so early?" asked James, ruffling Connor's hair and giving Prince a hearty pat.

"We wanted to see you off, and I want to ask you something special?" began the small boy.

James sat on the stool opposite Connor, looking serious. "I know what it is. You want me to bring you back a cowboy hat, don't you? Don't worry, I won't forget."

Connor gave a faint smile, and shook his head. "No, that's not it, Mr Young. I just want you to bring back my Dad. I miss him."

The flight to Alicante gave James time to think carefully about his next move, as well as the implications of what they had discovered. The revelation that Connor was Sam's son was akin to stoking a hornet's nest in the village. James recalled the horrendous events of three years earlier …

James shivered as he recalled a conversation with Peggy Skinner, Lady Lotitia's devoted maid, and her predictions of events that were to follow. He still clearly remembered her troubled face and the whispered words of "You are not here by accident" as she sought him out during one late evening at the Manor House. The events that followed would haunt him for the rest of his life.

Sam Rivers was, as most people who knew him would agree, a cunning, spiteful but highly intelligent and handsome young man. He could be immensely charming when he wished, and his long, straw coloured hair, piercing, bright blue eyes and dusky skin that made him highly attractive to both women and men alike. Sam was very athletic, with a wiry, but muscular build, that gave him amazing strength. People often commented that Sam appeared to be made of rubber, as he could twist and contort his body into shapes that most people would think impossible for the human body. James remembered the many school sports trophies that had Sam Rivers' name inscribed on them, as well as entries in the school log book that confirmed his amazing athletic prowess. Sadly, instead of turning these amazing skills to good use on the sports field, Sam decided that another route was such more entertaining and profitable.

In Prior's Hill School, Sam mimicked his school classmates with ease, and James recalled entries in the old school log book where Sam had been punished for doing so. As he grew older, Sam would skilfully impersonate both men and women for profit and quickly realised that this, together with his acrobatic and escapologist skills, could usefully be deployed into a life of profitable crime.

As a teenager, Sam was involved in petty crime, and quickly became the scourge of the village. He also had another well-developed skill as an impersonator, which he honed to perfection. Sam could mimic and impersonate any man or woman with considerable accuracy and skill; many villagers were deceived by hoax telephone calls that were eventually tracked down to Sam Rivers, who was testing his developing skills for amusement and, later, considerable profit.

It was regarded as common knowledge in Prior's Hill that, as a child, it was Sam who was responsible for the death of his adoptive father, John Rivers, by leaving him to die a slow and painful death, impaled upon metal railings outside the cottage where they lived. It was also generally assumed that Sam was later responsible for the death of his adoptive mother, Rita Rivers, as he was impatient to get his hands on the money that she had saved so carefully over many years. Sam's links to both deaths were never proven, but this minor detail would never stop people gossiping about Sam Rivers within the close-knit Prior's Hill community. Needless to say, this young man was disliked, and villagers were ashamed of him.

After Tristan had been so tragically killed, it was Sam Rivers who tormented the grieving James by impersonating him and pretending that he had come back from the dead. James had often wondered if it was Sam who had planned the death of Tristan of whom he was so jealous. The police had considered this possibility, but nothing was proven. Following

Tristan's untimely death, Sam appeared a number of times to both James and Doris, and James admitted that Sam looked very much like his beloved Tristan. He would sometimes admit to himself that he briefly became attracted to Sam as a replacement for Tristan. This mutual attraction was a cruel ploy to force James into helping Sam to ingratiate himself with the Peatwhistle family, and Lady Lotitia in particular, that would lead to the eventual take-over of the Peatwhistle estate that Sam considered to be his birth right. James shuddered as he remembered that the reason why his Tristan and Sam Rivers looked so much alike was that they shared the same father, Grant Peters. It was later discovered that Sam had murdered his biological father in an act of planned revenge.

James, being a generous man towards others, always thought that, in fairness to Sam, the scene was set for tragedy long before Sam was born. Sam was the product of a brief, but heady relationship between a young Lady Lotitia Peatwhistle and a much younger, handsome lorry driver during a night of gin-induced passion. Lady Lotitia was bored with married life to her much older husband, Sir Toby, and her days were often filled with less than healthy distractions of gin, gambling and brief affairs with the opposite sex. Lady Lotitia's affair led to the birth of Sam, who was immediately shunted off to local estate workers, John and Rita Rivers, to be brought up as their own son. In turn, the couple were given generous financial inducements to keep the affair quiet, which they did until their deaths. Sir Toby was fully aware of the cover up, but refused to have anything to do with Sam Rivers.

Sam discovered the truth of the circumstances of his birth as a boy whilst playing with his friend, Giles, the Peatwhistles' son, in the Manor House. He was deeply resentful of his situation, and made it his mission to claim the Peatwhistle Estate that he saw as his birth right. He was nearly successful in poisoning Lady Lotitia, but his attempt at murder was discovered just in time by James, which again added to Sam's anger towards him. Tragic events three years ago nearly led to the death of Lady Lotitia and Sir Toby during an attempt upon their lives by Sam. Again, James intervened just in time, but was shot alongside his brave dog, Prince. Sam was arrested and charged with attempted murder, but then escaped. Nothing more had been heard from him until Connor had given James the letter the previous day.

Chapter 12

The heavy aircraft door opened, and James was anxious to get out of the crowded plane as quickly as he could. He disliked flying, and hated being in a cramped space next to people he didn't know. He felt the blast of hot air move through the cabin, as soon as the door opened and remembered that in Spain the summer heat could be challenging.

James was impatient to collect his luggage from the luggage belts. He had thought about travelling light with only hand luggage, but did not know how long he would be away. Thank goodness it is the summer holidays, he thought to himself. He had asked his deputy, Anne Armstrong, to keep an eye on the new building, and he knew that Cedric could always be relied upon to raise the alarm if there was a problem. Despite these reassurances, James still felt guilty that he would not be there to keep an eye on the building work.

James vaguely remembered Alicante Airport from his holiday in Benidorm many years earlier. He finally managed to locate his luggage and headed for the airport exit and the taxi rank outside. A taxi was already waiting, and the driver got out of the car, grabbed James' suitcase and put it in the back of the taxi. James handed details of the hotel where he was staying to the driver, who nodded and smiled. The driver opened the rear door, and James opened the rear passenger door, and James sat in the cigarette smoke-filled cab.

"Benidorm Old Town, Yes?"

"That's right," said James, pleased that the driver was able to speak some English. May I speak to you in English?"

"Yes, of course, amigo," began the driver. "I work on taxis for many years. I know you English, I know what you like."

James thought he saw the driver winking at him through the reverse mirror.

"You like nice sexy girls, or nice sexy boys? Andreas take you wherever you want to go. I very discreet too."

James smiled, as he thought that he would play Andreas at his own game.

"Actually, it's cowboys that I really like. Is there anywhere where I can find some?"

Andreas thought for a moment, looked puzzled, and then laughed, "Ah yes, amigo, you tease me. It's the cowboy show you want. It's a short drive outside Benidorm. I take you there tomorrow?"

"Yes, that would be good, Andreas. Please collect me from my hotel tomorrow."

"The show start at midday. I collect you at eleven. You give me money and I get ticket. I get you best seat in the house. I know Sheriff; he always give my friends best seats in house. It's very cheap and has real cowboy beer."

As James left the taxi, he thrust a handful of notes into Andreas' hand.

"I'll see you tomorrow then, at eleven o'clock," confirmed James to the grinning Andreas, who handed him his suitcase from the boot of the taxi.

"Adios, amigo. You have good day in beautiful Benidorm. I see you tomorrow. I find you sexy cowboys!"

James sighed as he walked up the steps to the quaint, traditional hotel that Christian had booked for him. He knew that he had been fooled once again, and doubted that he would see Andreas tomorrow, or ever again for that matter.

James had a restless night. He had telephoned Christian as he had promised, and also chatted briefly with Connor. Both were clearly worried about him and James could tell from Christian's voice that he was trying to warn him yet again without worrying Connor. James tried to be light-hearted, and told Connor that he was going to buy him a cowboy hat tomorrow.

"Tell Dad that I love him, and I miss him," was the last thing that Connor said, as the phone clicked off.

The hotel room and bed was comfortable enough, but he was restless as the events of the last few days played on his mind. The room was also unbearably hot, and James could not get cool even though the circular ceiling fan was on full speed. What if all this was another of Sam's meaningless games? What happens if Connor is taken away by social services after all the promises that he had made to the boy? He couldn't bear to let Connor down. Were Sam's pleas genuine or was it leading James into a dangerous situation as Christian had warned?

It was a hot and sunny morning. James had finally fallen into a deep sleep, but was sharply reminded of the difficult day that lay ahead when his alarm went off. He took a quick shower, and later went to the hotel's small breakfast room. He wasn't hungry, but enjoyed a large bowl of fresh fruit and several cups of delicious, steaming hot coffee. His mind went back to the last awful coffee that he had made for Cedric and himself at school. James made up his mind to invest in a decent coffee machine for the school staff room when he got home. Coffee in Spain was just so good.

After breakfast, James wandered into the town. Surprisingly, nearly all the shops were still closed. He remembered that in Spain, people work, eat and play into the small hours, because days begin late and end in the early hours of the following morning. After exploring the quaint, narrow streets for a few minutes, James spotted a small shop where an elderly woman was removing the shutters. He went up to her and asked, "Do you have any cowboy hats?"

The old woman shook her head and waved her hands. James realised that of course, she didn't understand what he was saying. How arrogant of him to assume that everyone understood English.

The old woman beckoned him inside the now open shop. It was far larger on the inside than outside, as the shop was surprisingly long and narrow. James was delighted to see a fancy dress and carnival section that held an excellent selection of hats on the shelves above the clothes racks. There were hats for clowns, sailors, soldiers and there was even a British bobby's hat, complete with a small Union Flag stuck on the front. At the end of the shelf was an impressive selection of cowboy hats, or Stetsons, as they were labelled. James selected one that was clearly for a sheriff, and sensibly chose the small size for Connor.

He handed it to the elderly woman, who smiled, as she took the money and placed the hat in a large bag. "For son?" she asked. James thought for a moment, nodded and smiled as he left the shop, deep in thought.

At precisely eleven o'clock, Andreas and his taxi appeared. James must have looked surprised, since Andreas looked concerned when he spotted James coming towards him.

"Good morning, amigo. You surprised to see me? I told you that I would be here. We Spanish are good people; we late sometimes, but always arrive in the end," he laughed.

"No problem," smiled James. "I had no doubt that you would be here. You are very prompt, which I appreciate."

"Good, amigo. Now I find some beautiful cowboys to enjoy."

Chapter 13

The bright yellow taxi sped out of the crowded town and into the beautiful mountains surrounding Benidorm. Although James had visited the town many years earlier, it never ceased to amaze him how the tall and often weirdly designed, modern buildings looked strangely beautiful and comfortable against the traditional, natural landscape that surrounds the town. He had heard Benidorm described in equal measure of both approval and disapproval. Since Benidorm was one of the most successful tourist destinations in Spain, he felt that the town had rather a lot going for it.

The taxi was soon negotiating potholes and unmade roads as it skirted around the town and sped higher into the mountains. They soon came across a large sign, painted with the words 'Dodge City', which had a picture of a grinning cowboy and a dead Indian, at which point Andreas excitedly stabbed his finger in the air.

"That's where we go," he almost shouted at James as they entered what appeared to be a huge ravine.

James nodded, "How long has it been open? I've never heard of it before."

"It's always been here, I think. It's an old film set where they made cowboy films. The film people left, and it became tourist attraction a few years ago," replied Andreas, turning around to James, and at the same time the taxi hit a nasty pothole in the unmade road.

For the first time, James noticed what a handsome young man his driver was with his jet black, curly hair and brilliant white teeth. His partly unshaven face added to the attraction, and James could see from his tight-fitting top and muscular arms that he 'worked out'.

The taxi finally pulled into a rough, unmade car park, and a stopped between a group of cars in an area that appeared to be free of potholes and lumps of rock. It was indeed a beautiful setting, and as James stepped out of the car, he looked admiringly at the town below. They were some way up the mountain road it seemed, and Benidorm looked perfect set against a clear, blue sky.

James and Andreas joined the long queue of visitors that lined up outside the shed that served as a booking office. "You don't have to wait with me," said James. "You could give me the ticket and maybe you could pick me up later? I don't know what time the show ends."

"Oh, I come with you, amigo," grinned the handsome Spaniard. Sheriff say I have free entry, because I bring you. I not seen show for many years, and they say it's really good. It was on news, as they have serious accident. It even more popular now because of accident."

'Dodge City' was enclosed by a very tall wooden fence, which hid all that lay inside. When they reached the booking office, a young woman looked at their two tickets, stamped them hard with a rubber stamp and indicated that they should go through the pair of tall gates.

"Wow," exclaimed James, "this is incredible. It's a real cowboy town!"

On each side of the dusty unmade road were lines of wooden buildings, including shops, stables, bars, a Sheriff's office, prison building and a collection of other buildings. Some were complete buildings that visitors could enter, whilst others were merely shells that served the purposes of a film set, James guessed. Horses wandered along the road, together with cowboys laughing, drinking and tending their horses.

Andreas grinned with appreciation.

"We go bar now. I have seats and we watch from outside. Visitors no book watch show from road, but we have best seats and beer."

The two men were soon seated on less than comfortable wooden benches, and a buxom 'serving wench', as was described on the information sheet, dressed in cowboy appropriate, breast-revealing costume, appeared with two large glasses of beer. James gratefully sipped the beer. It was already a very hot day and temperatures had risen rapidly since they had arrived at 'Dodge City'.

There was a general hush and air of expectation. Visitors suddenly became very quiet and walked quickly to the side of the road as they excitedly awaited the start of the performance. Cowboys, 'wenches' and other participants took their positions along the road, whilst horses contentedly munched on the feed given to them.

The township lay in a dusty ravine and, despite a few clouds in the brilliant blue sky, it was an airless day and everything seemed as dry as dust. A few dogs were barked in the distance, the occasional rider stopped outside the store and tethered his horse before escaping from the heat. There was an air of dreaded expectancy in the township; this was the day that they had been waiting for and dreading. It was the day when Big Jake was due in town and the stench of death was already in the air.

The saloon bar was busy. It seemed as if the townsfolk sensed that there was safety in numbers, or maybe it was just an unspoken wish that they should all spend their last day together. The bartender looked nervously at the clock on the wall. It would soon be time. He started nervously stacking away the empty glasses beneath the bar, and removing bottles from the shelves behind him.

The thunder of horses' hooves entering the small township made the townsfolk feel uneasy. Those that were outside scuttled into the saloon or back to their homes to escape the coming tensions and ultimate showdown. A cloud of dust appeared in the distance, as horses and riders reached the outskirts of this quiet town. A small boy stood, transfixed outside the General Store.

The air was heavy with expectation. The birds stopped singing, and the gentle neighing of horses resting outside the blacksmith stopped, as they too shuffled their hooves nervously. There came a thunderous sound, as a group of six horses and their riders burst into the village like a hurricane. The leader of the group, a big, fat unshaven man with heavy sideburns and moustache, leapt from his horse.

"Where is the little runt? I'll put a bullet through anyone I finds hiding him here! Do yer hear me!"

Any townsfolk who were watching the entry of Jake and his pose of criminals suddenly melted away. They disappeared into homes, shops or anywhere where they would not be noticed. The small boy continued watching by the door of the General Store. No one seemed to notice him or be concerned about his safety.

"I knows you're all in there!" Jake bawled through the door of the saloon. "You got five seconds to hand him over, or me and my mates will blow up the whole building, with you lot inside!"

"There's no threatening going on in my town, Mister," came a voice from outside the Sheriff's office. The Sheriff, a tall, burley man, wandered to the group of riders, gun in hand "You throw your gun down, and walk over here, real quiet. We got you covered, so you comes real quietly."

The Sheriff fell to the ground as a well-placed bullet shot through his head and he fell to the dusty ground. There were screams from some of the women watching through the windows and doors of the saloon bar. The small boy watched, but with no expression on his young face.

———

"Right. That's a taster of what my men's gonna do to all of you unless you hand him over. Me and my men will shoot all of you, and raise this miserable town to ashes. You got another five seconds."

"Five, four, three, two..."

"I'm here, Jake. Don't touch these people. It's not their fault. They are innocent of my crimes. Just let them all go in peace. I'm over here," came a voice from the roof of the General Store.

"Ah, you's seen sense at last, Blondie. Just come over here to your Uncle Jake. I gotta surprise for you!" boomed the big man.

A slim, blonde young man, slipped down from the roof of the General Store, with the easy and grace of a gymnast. He walked slowly to his tormentor, as the townsfolk once again started to appear from their doorways. They watched in awe at the grace and composure of the handsome young man with the long blond hair. The townsfolk began to clap, as he slowly approached Jake.

"Strip the little runt," ordered Jake. "Check him for sudden surprises. You know what happened last time. This one likes to play games, don't you, Blondie? This time, there'll be no escaping, as its time to meet your maker!"

Two of the five remaining men grabbed the young man and roughly ripped off his dusty jacket, blood stained shirt, trousers and worn boots. The young man was left standing in nothing more than his grubby grey pants. The crowd watched in silence, as they caught sight of the handsome, yet defiant stranger standing in their midst. He was someone that they had accepted and welcomed into their small community. They knew what would happen next. The small boy began to shake and then to sob loudly. Jake walked over to the terrified child, cuffed him with the back of his hand and the small boy stumbled.

"Don't you dare hit the kid! You pick a fight with me, but not the kid. That's the coward's way, Jake, and you knows it! You leave him alone."

Jake hit the terrified boy yet again, but this time harder and with the edge of his gun. The terrified child cried and fell to the ground. Jake kicked and spat at him, as he wandered over to the young man whose hands and feet were now bound with coarse rope.

"I'll do want I want with that bloody kid, after I've finished with you! You can either tell me where you stashed it and I'll blow your brains out real quick, or you can stay silent and I'll blow your balls off, and wait a while before I blow your brains out. Either ways it's not gonna be a pretty sight," snarled Jake.

The young man said nothing. He stood defiantly glaring at the man who was about to take his life away. There were was one shot, together with a long pause as the young man fell to the ground, and writhed and screamed in agony. The second shot brought peace and silenced the screams, as the beautiful young man with the bright blonde hair became surrounded by a pool of blood.

James felt a shiver sweep across his very being, he started to shake and sob uncontrollably; he groaned as he slumped to the ground …

Chapter 14

James woke up in the crowded saloon bar. He was lying on an old, leather couch with his head propped up on a cushion.

"I think we need an ambulance," said a voice, "I reckon he's had a heart attack."

Through blurred and wet eyes, James could see Andreas standing anxiously over him.

"You OK, Señor James? You well? I get doctor for you?"

"No, no. I'll be OK", mumbled James.

He could also see Big Jake and the Sheriff standing by Andreas, as well as a host of other cowboys and 'wenches' peering anxiously over him.

"Hmm, well you stay here quietly and drink that brandy. That'll sort you out better than any medicine man, I promise you that", said the burley Sheriff, with a grin. "We frightened the hell out of you, didn't we? Sorry about that, but it shows how good our acting is, doesn't it?

James gave a feeble laugh. "Yes, I guess it does. I'm so sorry to have been such a nuisance. I don't really remember what happened, other than it was very hot. I think I passed out. How long was I out for and how did I get here?"

"Not long," boomed the Sheriff. "You fell and Andreas here called for help. Big Jake and Andreas carried you in here. It was actually very good, because the crowd thought you were part of the act. You got a huge clap when you were carried into the saloon! How about doing a repeat performance tomorrow? I'll pay you well."

"I'm pleased I was of some help then," James smiled, as he tried to get to his feet.

"No hurry, young man. You stay here with Andreas. I've just got to finish the show, and then we'll have a chat to make sure you are feeling better. Can you stay with him, Andreas?" asked the Sheriff.

"No problem. We drink brandy here."

"Not you, Andreas. Remember you are driving me back to the hotel, and I didn't like the look of those cliff edges," interrupted James.

"OK, OK, you are spoil sport," grinned Andreas." I'll have juice to wash down the one I've had. It was for shock, amigo."

Sometime later, the Sheriff reappeared. "How are you feeling?"

"Much better now, thank you," replied James., "but I have many questions to ask you."

"Yes, I guessed that," nodded the Sheriff. "Where do you want to start?"

"Do you know someone called Sam Rivers?" began James, "I think he works here. I thought it was him in the play today. The young man who was shot, is that Sam?"

The Sheriff shook his head sadly.

"I'm afraid not. It is true that Sam Rivers worked here, indeed, for several years and for a few weeks at a time. I'm sorry to tell you that Sam died, and we think murdered, several weeks ago. I guess he was a friend of yours, and I'm so sorry to have to tell you this," said the burly man, kindly.

James thought and hesitated for a moment before replying, "I guessed as much, which is probably why I passed out, but what happened?"

"Sam used to work for us for a few weeks each year. He would never stay long as he had a young kid to look after in England, but he was very popular and we all liked him. We mostly take it in turns to play the different roles, but I don't think Big Jake and I would be convincing enough as the innocent young man, do you? Anyway, Sam and three other guys used to take turns in being the young guy who gets shot. Sam would do anything; he used to work in the snake pit, work the trapeze, climb and dive off the prison roof into a burning building. You name it, Sam was up for it; he was so athletic with a body that seemed to be made of stretch rubber. Anyway, one day it was Sam's turn to be the young man who gets shot. We use blanks, of course, but this time Sam got shot for real, right though the chest. You see, it was a real bullet and it killed him instantly."

James swallowed hard, "What happened to the guy who was playing Big Jake?"

"Paul was arrested for murder, but was later released, as the police now think the bullet was swapped just before the show, which Paul was unaware of. We didn't ask Paul back to the show, just in case. It was big news over here at the time, which is why we now have huge crowds visiting to see the show. Macabre really, isn't it? The police are still making enquiries, so we hope whoever did it gets caught and is punished."

James nodded, as yet more pieces of the jigsaw seem to be falling in place. "I came to see Sam, as we are looking after his boy. What happened to Sam's body? Is there anyone else I can speak to?"

Big Jake stepped forward, "I think you should have a chat with Goldie. He is a sort of lawyer, but was struck off for money laundering. He still does some work in the Old Town, and I know that Sam and he became friends. After Sam died, Goldie seemed to take care of everything."

"You give me Goldie's address?" asked Andreas, "I take Señor James to him."

James looked quizzically at Andreas and wondered once again how he knew his name.

"Be careful with that guy," warned Big Jake. "I think he's OK, but I know that he got mixed up with the Mafia at one stage, which is why he was struck off as a lawyer."

James got up to leave the saloon bar with Andreas. Surprisingly, as James held out his hand to shake hands, the burly Sheriff and Big Jake both hugged him. "You take care of Sam's boy, won't you? Oh, just one more thing. You must take this with you."

The Sheriff disappeared into a side room and reappeared with a large Stetson. "This is the hat that Sam always wore when he played the kid who got shot. Telling the boy that his father is dead will be difficult enough for you, but give him this hat as a reminder of his father. In time, it might help a little."

Once again holding back his tears, James gratefully took the Stetson from the Sheriff, said a final goodbye to the saloon bar staff, and walked out of Dodge City to Andreas' taxi for the return drive, and the relative normality of Benidorm, or so he thought.

Chapter 15

On the journey back to Benidorm, James reflected on the day's developments. At last, he knew what had happened to Sam, but felt uncomfortable, as he also knew that the true events were very similar to the nightmares that he had suffered from over the last few years. He did not understand how this could be, but planned to discuss this with Christian when he returned home. James began to wonder if he needed psychiatric help himself, and this deeply troubled him.

James also could not understand how Andreas knew his name. It was true that Andreas had been exceedingly helpful to him the previous day, but how did he know his name? Andreas was certainly going out of his way to befriend and support him, but why?

"Andreas?" asked James,

"Yes amigo?"

"How do you know my name? I didn't tell you, but you seemed to know it," questioned James.

"Oh, that's easy, Señor James. "You told me when you woke from big sleep."

"When I fainted? Did I?"

"Oh yes," nodded Andreas. "You did."

They soon arrived back at James' hotel. Andreas stepped out of the car.

"Tomorrow I take you to Goldie. I here early, and you fly back to England maybe?"

"That's a good idea," agreed James, suddenly wondering how did Andreas know that he was flying home the following evening.

"Andreas, would you like to have a meal with me tonight?"

The handsome taxi driver smiled, "Yes, that is good. I like know more about you, Señor James."

"As I would you, Andreas," agreed James.

"I collect you at 8.00 pm, Mr James, and I take you for good meal."

After a short nap, James telephoned Christian and Connor to tell them about his day, but he missed out most of the detail, as he considered that it would worry them too much. James ordered a drink and waited in the hotel lobby for Andreas to collect him. Andreas arrived exactly on time, but this time he hugged James before walking over to the hotel desk. He said something in Spanish to the receptionist, who smiled and made a note in the diary on her desk.

"I make booking for another English friend. Did I tell you my Uncle own hotel? He give me money if I bring guests."

James nodded and the two young men stepped out in the warm, sultry night-time air.

"I take you to small restaurant owned by member of my family," grinned Andreas. "I have big family and they into many things."

Andreas and James chatted and made small talk until they entered a small, cosy restaurant, where Andreas was greeted with affection by a beaming, middle aged woman.

"This is Aunt Maria, James," announced Andreas, hugging the beaming woman. "She know everything in Benidorm. She is, how you say, very nosey," he laughed, touching his nose.

Aunt Maria clearly knew what Andreas was saying, as she gave Andreas a gentle smack across his face.

"Ouch, you hurt me!"

Aunt Maria nodded and smiled knowingly, as she showed James and her nephew to a small table in the window of the restaurant.

"You want drinks?" she asked.

Andreas nodded and ordered in Spanish, "Is wine OK for you Señor James? I order good bottle of vino tinto from Uncle's vineyard."

James laughed, "That's perfect, Andreas, thank you. You certainly seem to have family everywhere."

James and Andreas continued making polite conversation until the wine had been delivered, poured and their meals ordered. James noticed 'Sanchez' written across the label, and assumed that was Andreas' family name. He pointed at the label, and Andreas grinned, and nodded.

"This restaurant has a surprisingly good vegetarian menu, Andreas. I am a vegetarian, so it is very unusual to see such a choice in Spain. I will enjoy eating here. Thank you for bringing me."

Andreas paused before he blurted out, "Señor James. I have confession."

James paused from drinking his wine, put the glass down and looked carefully at Andreas.

"Go on. It's what I asked you earlier, about my name, isn't it? Speaking of names, this wine of your Uncle's is very good."

Andreas nodded, "Yes, I sorry, I tell you truth. I know Señor Christian very well. He was my lover many years ago."

James picked up his glass again, and took a large sip, "Go on?"

"Señor Christian came to Benidorm many years ago. We work in bar together. We become good friends, and then lovers. He had no money, so he lived with my mother and me for few months. He then left and I not see him again."

James nodded, he had expected worse, much worse. "Is your mother's name, Maria?" he asked.

Andreas looked surprised and nodded, "Yes, how you know?"

James laughed, "Because every year, Christian goes to the florist in Abbotsford to send a lady called Maria a bouquet of flowers through Inter-flora. It's always at Christmas and he says it's for his Aunt. I got very jealous the first time he did it, because I thought it was maybe for another lover."

Andreas nodded and laughed too. "I see. Yes, Señor Christian send flowers to my mother every Christmas. He love my mother and she love him too; they were good friends. They stay in contact, but I not hear from Señor Christian for many years, until few days ago."

James listened carefully, as he topped both his and Andreas' glasses with wine.

"Señor Christian telephone my mother and say he need my help. He knew I taxi driver and ask where I work. My mother gave my number and he call me. He said you were in serious danger and want me to look after you. He want me to find safe place to stay and keep an eye on you. He told me about Connor. I promise I help you. He love you very much Señor James. He is very good man."

Not for the first time that day, James' eyes began to fill with tears. He put his hand on Andreas' arm that was resting on the table.

"All this now makes sense, and I thank you, Andreas. You are being a wonderful friend to both of us, and I couldn't have done without your help today."

"Maybe one day you came again to Benidorm as family? You bring Connor as well? My mother would love to see Señor Christian again, and they will never stop talking!"

"I would like that very much, Andreas, but tell me how did you know that I'm a vegetarian? Is this just a coincidence, or did Christian have something to do with it?"

Andreas beamed a toothy smile, "Yes, he told me and I asked my Aunt to prepare special vegetarian menu for you. Señor Christian told me that you don't eat when you are stressed, and he want you have good meal, so here we are!"

James and Andreas enjoyed their evening together, as James told Andreas about his and Christian's life in Prior's Hill, and the story of Sam Rivers and his son, Connor. Andreas was a good listener too, and James noticed how much happier he felt after he had shared his story. When the time came to leave, James offered to pay Aunt Maria for the meal.

"No, amigo. I want give you good time to relax. I promise Christian. Tomorrow will be difficult day for you."

"Difficult?" asked James, sounding concerned.

"I ask around about Goldie. I not know him, but I know people who do. He wasn't, how you say, 'struck off' being a lawyer for nothing. It is important we very careful."

Chapter 16

At ten o'clock precisely, Andreas appeared in the small hotel foyer, where James was waiting. Andreas greeted James with a big hug that took James by surprise.

"You feel better today, amigo?" enquired Andreas.

"Much better, thank you. I really want to get this visit to Goldie over and done with. I'm a bit worried about it, and I have many questions to ask him. Can you come in with me please, because I don't know if he speaks English? I hope he will see us, as I haven't made an appointment."

"He speak perfect English. Goldie born in Spain, but live in England for many years. I think he went to England university, but came to Spain to become lawyer. There should not be a problem, but I come in office with you. He will see you. I call him yesterday to make sure."

James smiled with gratitude at the young man walking beside him. "Thank you, Andreas. I don't know how I would manage all this without you."

Andreas took James on the brief journey through a series of narrow streets in the Old Town to Goldie's office. It was an old, unassuming building with a bar on the ground floor, and a series of offices on the floors above. James peered at the weather-worn, brass name plates displaying the names of the various office occupants.

"That him," said Andreas, stabbing the bottom plate with his finger, "Hugo Garcia-Perez, Assessor, That him."

James and Andreas entered a narrow, dark corridor that led to a warren of small offices at the rear of the building. James knocked on a partly open door that had the word 'Assessor' on the wall.

An attractive woman came to the door, and smiled warmly.

"Come in. Señor Perez is waiting. First, you must pay me five thousand pesetas, which will cover cost of your first consultation. You may pay by cash or card," she added pointing to a credit card machine sitting on her desk.

"No, I am not paying anything until I have met Mr Perez," said James, crossly.

Andreas intervened with a babble of Spanish, to which the young woman grimaced, and knocked on the door of the adjoining office. There was a pause, the young woman reappeared, smiled and opened the door for James and Andreas to enter.

A short, plump man with a fast receding hairline came towards them, and held out his hand towards James, but ignored Andreas.

"Good morning, Mr James. I am so pleased to see you. As you know, I am Señor Perez, but everyone calls me Goldie, I don't know why," he laughed. "Do please call me Goldie."

James nodded and shook his hand. Goldie was indeed true to his name. The short plump figure was adorned with a thick, gold necklace, one large gold earring, a heavy, expensive looking gold watch and a gold chain bracelet. He smiled at James, revealing one shiny, gold tooth.

"Before we sit down and discuss your problem, we will go and see Mr Sam. He is waiting for you next door."

James felt his legs go weak, and his face drained of colour, as he glanced at Andreas."

"It's happening all over again. Just as I thought; it's yet another of Sam's tricks, Andreas, I know it."

Andreas looked concerned and took his friend's arm, "I here, James. Don't worry."

Goldie looked concerned too, "Is your friend ill?" he asked glancing at Andreas for the first time. "You come in this room, and I will explain everything. I know this is distressing for Mr James."

James and Andreas followed Goldie into a small room, which would be best described as a small walk-in cupboard. On one of the shelves, that was littered with box files and legal books, sat a funeral urn."

"There we are," announced Goldie, with some pride and a flourish of his left arm. Here is Sam. Such a pity what happened to him. I hope you will take him home with you, Mr James? He does not belong here."

James felt a rush of relief as they left the tiny room with Goldie carrying Sam's ornate urn, which he placed on his desk with a heavy thud. "You sit down, Mr James, and I will get another chair for your friend."

Goldie left the office to get another chair, and Andreas rubbed James' arm. "It's OK, James. Everything OK."

Goldie returned with another uncomfortable looking wooden chair and beckoned for Andreas to sit on it. Goldie returned to his comfortable looking, black leather swivel chair on the other side of the desk.

"I am pleased you came to see me. I have many things to give you and to talk about, Mr James."

"I too have many questions, Goldie. First, how did you know Sam Rivers. Why did he come to you?"

Goldie thought for a moment before answering, feeling a little uncomfortable. He had met people like James before. This is a man who asked very direct questions and demanded direct answers, he thought.

"I will tell you all, Mr. James, but you must be patient with me as there is a lot to tell, and some painful memories for me too. I met Mr Sam when he first came to Benidorm some years ago. He worked for me in a club that I also own in the Old Town. Do you know 'The Black Cat Club'? We have drag artistes, and dancers. It's a lot of fun, you should come one night."

"Thank you, but I'm leaving Spain later today. What did Sam do for you?"

"He was a barman at first, and a very good one; everyone liked him. His real talent was mimicry. He used to mimic customers, which we all thought was very funny; his observations and attention to detail were amazing. However, Sam being Sam, stepped over the line by mimicking me in a phone call to my manager and told the staff that we were closed for the evening. That little trick cost me a lot of money," frowned Goldie.

James nodded thoughtfully, "Yes, he was very good at that, as I also know to my cost."

"I was going to sack him for that incident," continued Goldie, "I then remembered that we were one drag queen short for the weekend, and asked Sam if he could step in. Sam immediately agreed and said he had done similar work in England. Well, to cut a long story short, Sam was amazing, a real natural. He became the talk of the town, and punters couldn't get enough of him."

"I thought he worked 'Dodge City' for the last few years?" asked James.

"He did, but that came later. Meanwhile, Sam became known throughout Benidorm. In fairness, he always gave 'The Black Cat Club' priority for bookings, but if we didn't need him, he would work for other bars and shows in town. He became very popular, because unlike most Spanish drag queens, he didn't mime the words of songs, he actually sang them. He had a wonderful voice; his Shirley Bassey was unbelievable. I must show you a short film of his performance one day."

James nodded, and kept glancing at the urn on Goldie's untidy desk. "What do you want me to do with that?"

"As you wish, but I suggest you take Sam home to Carlos, his son. Sam needs to have a proper funeral, and this will provide closure for his son."

"Connor. He's called Connor," interrupted James.

Chapter 17

Goldie opened a thick, brown file and shuffled through a sheaf of papers. "I think you will find that the boy is called Carlos, Mr James. Look."

Goldie handed an impressive looking document to James. It was all written in Spanish, and so James handed it to Andreas, who nodded."

"Yes, James, Goldie right. This is birth certificate. The boy is Carlos Connor Rivers-Sanchez."

"So Connor is Spanish? Sam is his British father and he has a Spanish mother," James said slowly. "Who was the mother? I know she died when Connor was very young."

"It says mother is Ana Dolores López Sanchez," replied Andreas, carefully scrutinising the document." Don't worry, James," he grinned, "Sanchez is my name too, it is very common, like the English 'Smith' name."

Goldie continued, "Carlos was born after a brief liaison between Sam Rivers and Ana, who was a dancer at my club. Everyone thought Sam was gay, but as we later found out, Sam was ambidextrous, he went both ways."

James smiled, as realised that Goldie had used the wrong word, but he knew exactly what Goldie meant; Sam liked both men and women.

"They lived together briefly for a while after the baby was born. Sam provided money for Ana and supported her and the baby quite well financially, but they didn't get on, and Sam was rarely seen with her or the baby. Sadly, when the child was old enough, Ana wanted a job and came to me for work, but I had none to give her at that time. She got a part-time job at the circus as a dancer, but also had to do some work on the trapeze. One night she fell, and was very badly injured, and died several days later."

"What happened to Connor, or Carlos?" interrupted James impatiently.

"Ana had no family that we knew of, so the neighbours looked after the boy for a few days. When I heard what happened, I contacted Sam who had returned to England to see his grandmother. He came back right away and took the baby back to England. I think his grandmother looked after the boy for a few years. I understand that she died recently?"

James nodded, "Yes, this is all fitting into place."

"Sam would regularly return to Benidorm, but always stayed longer in the summer. He was very popular, and was in high demand. He also worked at 'Dodge City', which he loved and it was a change for him not to be always in a dress as a female impersonator; he made a lot of money too. You can still see posters around the town advertising the amazing drag queen, 'Jennifer Miranda'; she was amazing and both men and women would fall in love with her. She was just so sexy and seductive, if you know what I mean?"

Goldie's gold tooth gleamed in the beam of sunlight as he winked.

James nodded, and shuddered as he remembered. "Yes, I know exactly who Jennifer Miranda is. I had the misfortune to dine with her one evening, but that's another story."

"Sam asked me to help him to ensure that his son would always be well provided for," continued Goldie. "I looked after Sam's money, as he was very bad at organising things like that, and I recently made a will for him, and you and Carlos are the main beneficiaries, Mr James. You see, Sam knew that he would not have a long life, and that he had to make provision for the boy."

"Where do I come in? Why did Sam want me to look after his son?"

"That's a mystery for me too. I guess he simply trusted you. He didn't have any remaining family that bothered about him, as I understand it, after his grandmother died. He had many friends over here, but none that he seemed to trust. Sam was a very clever and intelligent man, often deceitful, cunning and certainly a very good liar, but he could also be most charming and get away with anything. He was also incredibly handsome, and everyone fell in love with him. Not everyone trusted him though, and he made quite a few enemies simply because his act was so popular. There was a lot of jealousy."

"Do you know how he was killed?"

"Yes, I have the police report. They think it was murder, as a blank bullet was replaced with a live bullet in the pistol used during the show at 'Dodge City'. There was an autopsy, the guy playing Big Jake was arrested and charged and later released. Big Jake didn't kill him, as he wasn't clever enough to do anything like that."

"So, Sam was murdered? Any idea who may have done this?" demanded James, who was now feeling a most uncomfortable mix of horror, sadness and anger.

"I have my suspicions," replied Goldie, ignoring James' stare. "I must be very careful about what I say now, and you must not repeat any of this; for reasons that you will soon understand."

James nodded in agreement. "Go on."

"I used to own several bars in town," began Goldie. "Some were for our straight visitors, and others were for the gay men that visit our town each year. I had a very good business and made a lot of money. I was forced into a protection racket by the Mafia who operate on the Costa Blanca; Russian Mafia, that is. At first, I refused to pay, but the threats and intimidation forced me to accept their demands, so I had to launder money for them through the bars and clubs that I owned. Their money came mainly from prostitution, drugs, and their protection racket."

"That's dreadful," began James, "but what does this have to do with Sam?"

Goldie ignored James' interruption and continued his story, "When Sam was working for me at 'The Black Cat', he was seduced by another barman, who turned out to be one of the gang members. Sam fell for the guy, and he became sexually involved with him for several months. Basically, Sam was being groomed to help the gang with some of their work."

"What kind of work?"

"Well, for Sam, it was nothing too sinister; no murders or anything like that. As you know, Sam was very versatile. He was acrobatic, double jointed, and appeared to be made of rubber. He was amazingly agile, and could break into any building through physical effort, intelligence and cunning. The gang used him to break into expensive homes, offices and shops to steal valuable jewellery, documents - anything that they could use to blackmail their victims."

"Did Sam understand what was going on?"

"At first he thought it was bit of a game, but yes, I think he knew. Sam was vain, and always liked the attention he was getting; especially the praise, prestige and the money, which he was desperate to save for Carlos. He was naive in so many ways, but later he knew it was very serious."

"Was he caught?"

"No, surprisingly, he managed to give the police the slip on several occasions. As I said before, Sam was cunning and very clever. I guess the police are still looking for him, but the Mafia found him first; anyway, that's my theory."

James nodded, "I think you're right. Thank you for being so straightforward with me, Goldie, I appreciate it. Tell me, what happened to your involvement?"

"With the Mafia, you mean? Well, the police put a plant in the club, I was caught and prosecuted. I lost all my bars and clubs with the exception of 'The Black Cat'. I was fortunate to escape a lengthy prison sentence, but I cooperated with the police, and most of the gang were arrested. The Law Society stripped me of my status as a lawyer, and I am now reduced to running a small office as an 'Assessor'. You see how the mighty fall, Mr James?"

James nodded, "Are the Mafia still operating?"

Goldie nodded, sadly. "Oh yes, and getting stronger again across the Costa Blanca, the Costa del Sol and anywhere where there are tourists. They have mostly left me alone, as I am no more use to them, and they know that my activities continue to be closely monitored by the police. Sam was a different matter ..."

"Why is that?"

"They owed Sam a lot of money. He was promised great wealth for his contribution when he was working for them, but they didn't pay him. Sam swore that he would get what he was owed."

"And did he?"

"Oh yes, but I wish he hadn't," replied Goldie shaking his head. "Sam was determined he would get what he was owed. One of the last times that he came to see me, it was clear that he was up to something very serious. He wouldn't tell me what it was, as he thought I had already been in enough trouble. All I know, is that his bank account suddenly became very impressive, and that explains why the Mafia were determined to take him out."

"I understand now," said James, nodding. "What a frightening story."

"Listen to me, Mr James. You do what I say and keep Carlos away from all this. These people never forget. There is a lot of money and it's all waiting for Carlos. I have transferred the money to your Mr Carter, the lawyer in Abbotsford, I think," said Goldie, leafing through more papers. "It is a lot of money, and I suggest that you spend what you need for Carlos' education and other expenses, but put the rest safely into a trust fund for his future."

"I'm not spending any of Connor's money. As you suggest, it will be in a trust fund until he is twenty-one. How much are we talking about?"

"Good," nodded Goldie, retrieving another sheet of paper, a bank document, which he handed to James. "This is more or less what I've sent across so far; there's a bit more to be sent, less my expenses, cremation expenses and such like."

James took the piece of paper, and gasped, "This is ridiculous. What a huge sum of money! Did Sam rob a bank or something? Surely we cannot keep this?"

"The good Lord is the only one who knows that now," said Goldie, reverently crossing himself. "My best advice is to keep quiet. If we go the police with this, it will open up a huge can of worms, which could put you, Carlos and myself in great danger."

James nodded, "I understand, but this isn't right."

"I also want to give you other documents. You have Carlos' birth certificate. This is Sam's death certificate, which you will need if you adopt Carlos."

"I don't think I am allowed to adopt in the UK," began James.

"Of course you can, but only as a single man, but you cannot adopt Carlos as a same sex couple. Now, have a look at Sam's will." interrupted Goldie, handing over another impressive piece of paper to James, who in turn handed it to Andreas, who had been listening in amazement to the conversation.

"Sam's will is in Spanish, and I have an English translation," said Goldie, handing another large piece of paper to James. "It states that you or Christian are to be Carlos' adoptive parent. It asks that you adopt Carlos, but in the case of your demise, Christian would have that option too. The laws in Spain are different to England. I sent a copy of this will to Mr Carter who prepared a similar one under English law. Both have been signed by Sam and witnessed. I have registered the will in Spain, and so it is fully legal here, and I assume Mr Carter has done the same in England."

"What happens if I cannot adopt Connor? Maybe English law will not allow it?"

Goldie smiled, "That is why I suggested two wills, one for each country. If there is a problem in England, you move to Spain, and you will be Carlos' parent under Spanish law. It is easy and I can do it for you, for a small charge of course! You speak to Mr Carter when you get home, and take these documents with you. Oh, and this one too."

Goldie handed a Spanish passport to James. "I think Carlos was taken to England as a young child with a British passport, or maybe on his father's passport. I do not know for sure. Any more questions?"

James was sure that he would think of many more questions, but he shook his head, thanked Goldie, and both he and Andreas began to leave the small office.

"By the way, don't forget to give my secretary my consultation fee of five thousand pesetas when you leave. I'd be most obliged."

Chapter 18

After leaving Goldie's office, Sam and Andreas began the journey to Alicante airport. James was getting anxious, as the check in time would begin shortly. They talked about what had happened that morning, and James shared with Andreas his concerns about the unfinished business, as he saw it, and the money.

"I think Goldie right. You shake bee hive and bees come after you," said Andreas knowingly. James was sure that he was mixing metaphors, but knew what Andreas meant, and thought that he described their situation very well.

"So, what you do with that?" asked Andreas looking at the large, gaudy urn that James was carrying on his lap. James, who had previously only ridden in the rear seat of the taxi was now sitting next to Andreas in the front passenger seat, since Andreas had become a trusted friend.

James shook his head. "I'm not sure. At first, I thought I could scatter the ashes somewhere over here, but that doesn't seem right as Sam hasn't had a proper funeral. I owe it to Connor to take him home."

Andreas thought for a moment, "It difficult, but I agree. The boy should know what happened to father and remember him. You cannot take on plane. They will not allow."

"I thought I could fit it into my suitcase."

Andreas shook his head. "It not fit, amigo, but I have idea."

Andreas stopped the taxi outside a small supermarket. "You wait here."

A few minutes later, Andreas reappeared carrying a roll of black bin liners. "I know what to do. We put Sam in bin bags and I lose the urn. You understand?"

"We cannot do that," began James, "its, so, so disrespectful."

"You have better idea?" asked Andreas quizzically.

"OK then, let's do it."

Andreas took the urn and went to the back seat where he careful poured Sam's ashes into a black bin liner. He then double and triple bagged the large package, before proudly displaying it to James.

"There, Mr Sam quite comfortable in bag. I put in suitcase, and I take urn and put in bin. Be careful at check in. They think you carry drugs, so may be a problem." Andreas grinned as he saw James' face fill with concern at the thought of being prosecuted as a drug smuggler.

"I tease you, amigo. You are very easy to tease, Mr James. Don't worry, Mr Sam look like tea leaves and not drugs at all. You cannot go to prison for carrying tea leaves. No worries. Yes?"

The taxi arrived at the airport just as check in for James' flight opened. Andreas lifted James luggage from the boot, and handed the suitcase and the Stetson, which was now carefully wrapped, to James.

"I hope you and Mr Sam have good flight. Please give love to Christian and Connor. I hope you will all be very happy, and that one day you come to see Andreas again." Andreas gave James a big hug and kissed him on both cheeks.

"Thank you, Andreas. I will never forget your kindness, and I can never thank you enough. I can see why Christian liked you so much. Yes, we will come and see you one day, but why don't you and your mother come and see us and meet Connor? You can stay with us. I'm sure Christian would love to see you again, and it will save him sending flowers to your mother by Inter-flora, because she can collect them herself!"

Andreas smiled, and nodded. "Yes, we do that, amigo. You have good flight. I not forget you."

James took his suitcase and headed through the airport doors, and towards the check-in desks. He wondered if he would see Andreas ever again?

Chapter 19

As soon as James' taxi drew up outside Lavender Cottage, he could hear Prince barking very loudly. The front door opened and the enthusiastic dog almost flew out of the door, closely followed by Christian and Connor. Prince covered James with big, wet licks, whilst both Christian and Connor hugged James as he walked indoors.

"My goodness, what a wonderful welcome. I must go away again," laughed James.

"Oh no you don't," said Christian firmly. "Next time you decide to have a few lazy days in Spain, Connor and I are coming with you!"

"OK, it's a deal. I missed you all so much. I cannot wait to hear all your news. I seem to have been travelling all day, but it's not that long a flight. I guess it's all that hanging around in the airport, and sitting with nothing much to do."

Christian nodded, "Well, Connor and I have prepared a meal for you, if you are hungry, that is. Why don't you go upstairs and change into more comfortable clothes and relax? We've had our meal, but we will come and watch you eat Connor's stew."

Connor grinned, "Christian let me chop the vegetables, but he did all the flavourings."

"Well, I was a bit worried about the knife, but I thought that Connor had better get used to it as I want him to cook all our meals in future," teased Christian, ruffling Connor's hair.

"How's he been?" asked James, as soon as he was in the bedroom getting changed, and Christian had joined him.

"Very quiet and subdued for the last few days. Prince has been a great help, of course, but I've noticed that he cries and talks to Prince late at night. I can hear him in the bedroom, and I am never sure whether to go in and comfort him, or let him get it out of his system. In the end, I left it to Prince to deal with. I told Connor about Sam's death. He cried dreadfully at first, but we've talked about it quite a bit, not the details though, which I thought we could leave until he is a bit older."

James nodded, "Thank you, I'm pleased you told him; I was dreading that. He needs to know, of course, but we can tell him the rest later on."

"I had to go into work for a few hours yesterday, so Doris came to stay with Connor. She adores the boy and spoils him dreadfully. She played 'Scrabble' with him, which Connor loves, and he beat her twice. I thought that she had just let him win, but Doris assured me that she tried hard to beat him. You know how good she is at word games usually? I think we have a very clever little boy living with us."

James nodded as he changed his shirt, "I've no doubt about it, Chris. The good news is that, hopefully one day soon, we'll be able to call Connor our son, and give him the life that he deserves."

Over dinner, James gave a light-hearted account of his visit to Benidorm, his visit to 'Dodge City' and the people that he had met.

"I also met one of Christian's old friends, Andreas" began James, winking at Connor. "You wouldn't believe what he told me about Christian, Connor!"

Christian began to go bright red in the face, as he wondered what James was going to say in front of Connor. Connor started laughing.

"He asked if the three if us would like to visit him in Spain. Andreas is a really nice man, and I know you would like him, Connor. I also invited him and his mother to come and stay with us. They would be very welcome."

Connor nodded, "I would like to visit Spain one day."

"Did your Dad ever talk to you about Spain? I guess you have never been there?"

Connor shook his head, "No, never, but I've seen photos of the huge skyscrapers and beautiful scenery. Dad used to tell me about the cowboy city and how he liked working there. Sometimes, he would bring a costume or toy gun home to show me. He also sang in some bars and theatres there. He showed me photographs of his drag performances - he looked amazing, and very beautiful."

James nodded, "Yes, Connor. I heard about what an excellent performer he was, and how he gave people so much pleasure in the work that he did. One man I met said he was the most popular entertainer in Benidorm during the summer season. He was recognised as a brilliant performer."

Connor smiled proudly. "I wish I could have seen him doing that."

Later that evening, and after Connor had gone to bed, James went into his room to find the small boy quietly sobbing into his pillow. Prince was, as usual, at his side, looking concerned and occasionally giving him a lick of comfort. Connor stopped crying when he saw James sitting on the edge of his bed.

"It's OK to cry, Connor," said James, gently. "We would be very worried if you didn't cry at such sad news. I know how painful this is for you." He paused. "One day, I will tell you everything, as I made you a promise that there would be no secrets, but you will have to trust Christian and I to tell you things when we think you are ready. Do you understand what I am saying?"

The tear-filled boy looked at James, and nodded. "Yes, I understand, Mr Young. I am still very young and you are trying to protect me. I am quite tough really you know."

James smiled, "Yes, I'm sure you are, but we will all have a difficult few days ahead of us, so I want you to be very brave. I'm also going to give you something that may upset you at first, but I want you to think of it as a gift from your Dad who loved you very much."

James unwrapped the Stetson, and handed it to Connor. The boy's eyes widened, as he held it in his hands, "Is that for me? You said you would bring one back for me."

James nodded. "Actually, I did buy you one in Benidorm, and that one is still in my suitcase; you can have that tomorrow. This one is even more special because it belonged to your Dad. He had it with him when he died and so it belongs to you now. When you look at it, I want you to remember that whatever you may hear, your Dad loved you very much and did his best to protect and look after you. This is why he asked Christian and myself to look after you for him. This Stetson is to remind you of this."

Connor nodded, and more tears fell as he held James' hand.

"Thank you, Mr Young. I understand what you are saying. Yes, I will treasure this hat as a special present from my Dad."

"That's right. Now it really is time that you and Prince went to sleep. We have a busy day tomorrow. Goodnight Connor."

"Goodnight, Mr Young. I'm so pleased that you are home again. I feel safe here."

Chapter 20

The next day was certainly a very busy one. Christian had arranged to work at home during the morning, whilst James had business in Abbotsford. Connor had decided that the new railway layout was not good enough, so had asked if he could rearrange it entirely at the far end of the living room.

"Yes, of course you can, but don't we need more track? I can take you into town later and buy some more," said Christian.

James had already asked Christian to make an appointment with Mr Carter for when he returned home, as he had some urgent and serious business to discuss. This time, Jim Carter was much more cordial and welcomed James into his office.

"Good morning, Mr Young. I think I know why you are here. I am sorry that I was a little brusque with you on the telephone. I was bound to an agreement with my client, and I could not share matters with you at that stage. Since circumstances have changed, I am now at liberty to answer your questions and to help in any way that I can."

"It's about Sam Rivers and his son, Connor. I have been to Benidorm and found out what happened to Sam. I have also spoken to Goldie, that is Mr Perez, and he gave me some important papers to pass on to you.

Mr Carter smiled and nodded, "Yes, I have spoken to Mr Perez quite often recently. He appears to be quite a character, but does seem to know what he is doing. So, you have Mr Rivers' death certificate, Connor's birth certificate and Spanish passport? I assume that you also have a copy of Mr Rivers' Spanish will? I will give you a copy of the UK version, which is basically the same."

James passed all the documents to Mr Carter, who spent some time studying them.

"You are aware that Mr Rivers asked that you adopt his son, and the implications of this arrangement?"

James nodded.

"You are also aware that in the case of your incapacity or death, Mr Trill would be asked to adopt the boy, should he still be under age? He is happy with this also, I assume?"

"Yes, we are both aware. Ideally, we would like joint custody and adoption, but I know that is not possible."

"That is true, Mr Young. Maybe one day the law will be changed. I understand that things are moving quite fast in that direction within Europe, so one day it may be possible here. Until then, you can only adopt as a single man."

"How long will the adoption process take, Mr Carter?"

"Several weeks, or it could be months, Mr Young. I have already spoken to social services, and they seem confident that there will be no problems in your particular case. Of course, checks and enquiries will have to be made as to your suitability. I expect there will be several visits, and young Connor will need to be asked what he thinks as well."

James nodded, and felt much happier with the response and reassurance that he had heard.

Mr Carter paused, sat back in his chair and removed his glasses, "Are you also aware of the very large sum of money that Connor has inherited? Are you certain that this money has been acquired from fully legal sources?"

James paused, trying to be careful about his reply, as Goldie had asked. "I think some of the money was from Mr Rivers' success as an entertainer, as well as inheriting money from his grandmother when she died. Other than that, I have no idea where it came from."

"I see," began the cautious solicitor. "You see, money laundering is a very serious offence, both for yourself and myself as your solicitor. We must be clear that the finance was gained from impeccable sources."

"I really cannot add any more to this," began James. "Mr Rivers was a highly complicated man. Might I suggest that you speak again with Mr Perez, since he knew far more about Mr Rivers than both of us."

"Yes, I will do that, Mr Young. Meanwhile, how would you like the funds invested for Connor?"

"In a trust fund until he is 21 years old please, with myself, Mr Trill, Doris Cole and Lady Lotitia Peatwhistle acting as trustees. We will need to discuss the exact wording, in what circumstances each trustee acts, and how many signatures are required."

"Good, you seem to have thought about this in some detail already. Lady Lotitia indeed? Are you friends? Is she aware of her possible involvement?"

"Yes, she is fully aware of the Trust Fund that Mr Trill and I intend to establish for Connor, but no one other than Mr Trill and myself are aware of the large sum involved. We would like to keep it this way please."

Mr Carter nodded, "Yes, I am sure that would be possible. This sum of money will generate a very large interest. Would you like this paid into your own bank account to pay for the boy's day-to-day expenses, holidays, treats and such like?"

James shook his head. "No thank you. Connor will be treated as our son, and we will fund all his expenses. Leave the money to accrue, and we can forget about it until he is twenty-one."

"Well, that will certainly have become a very nice nest egg by then," smiled Mr Carter.

James' next visit was to see Paula at the undertakers, Brown and Co. James was surprised to see that since he had last been in town, the business had been renamed 'Cushion and De Valle, since as far as he knew, it had always been known as 'Brown and Co'. He remembered that the last time he had been inside the undertakers was when he had asked them to arrange the funeral of his beloved Tristan. His thoughts flew back many years to that tragic period in his life.

"May I help you, young man?" came a voice that he immediately recognised. It was Jasmine de Valle, their sometimes over enthusiastic friend, who immediately appeared from behind a large wooden desk and flung her arms around his neck, and then gave him a big kiss on the lips.

"Jasmine! How lovely to see you, but what are you doing here. You are supposed to be our librarian, not working at the undertakers!"

"Bit of a long story, actually, James," began Jasmine. "As you know, I worked in the library for many years, but it was always so quiet. I often used to think that it was like working in a morgue, so I thought I would actually work in one," screeched Jasmine.

James knew that Jasmine's long-term partner, Paula Cushion, or Paul Cushion, as Jasmine preferred to call her partner, was a mortician, so maybe this move for Jasmine made some sense. Although, he silently hoped that she could manage to tone down her often-outrageous behaviour.

"So, you and Paul have gone into business together? I noticed the signage has changed, and the entrance is lovely, bright and colourful. I remember it always being very dark and depressing."

"Exactly, James. You have it in one. I have always thought that funeral parlours should be bright and cheerful. Undertakers can often be so depressing, don't you think? After all, we are all going to fall off our 'perches' sometime, so we may as well as enjoy it, don't you think? 'Drop dead and enjoy it' is my motto!" Another ripple of excessive laughter encased the small parlour.

James nodded, "Well, you certainly have an interesting concept. Is Paul still here, working as a mortician?"

"Oh yes, she's back stage, and I'm front of house. I sell the ice creams and programmes, whilst Paul does the makeup, if you see what I mean?" guffawed Jasmine.

James couldn't help but notice that despite all the efforts to brighten the undertakers, a strong smell of formaldehyde still wafted from Jasmine's ample frame. He and Christian had often commented how the pervasive smell had lingered long after the couple had left their home following a visit.

"Jasmine, I need your help."

"My God, you've killed someone!"

"No Jasmine, but you've probably heard that we are looking after a young boy. His father was tragically killed and I wonder if you could help me to place his ashes into something more suitable?"

It was now James' turn to be outrageous, as he placed the black bin liner, stuffed with Sam's ashes on Jasmine's desk. For a moment, Jasmine seemed to be lost for words.

"Well, well I never! What a request indeed! Couldn't you have found something a little more appropriate, James? Maybe a Tupperware box?"

"Well, I had to squeeze him into my suitcase when I left Spain. I couldn't carry the urn that he came in."

Jasmine screeched with laughter so much that she had to sit down.

"I've never heard anything so outrageous! This will be a fabulous story to tell at our next Area Funeral Directors' Dinner" I cannot wait to tell them!"

"Well, hopefully you will be discreet and not mention my name ..." began James.

"Of course, of course. No, I'm sure Paul will have a nice urn somewhere in the back. When and where would you like it delivered?"

Chapter 21

James left his visit to Lady Lotitia Peatwhistle until late morning by which time he hoped that she should be ready to start her day. He had already telephoned the Manor House to ask if she would be in, but whoever took the call seemed unaware of her plans for the day. James decided that he would call anyway, as what he had to tell her could not wait.

It was Lady Lotitia's loyal maid, Peggy, who opened the large heavy door, rather than the butler who had retired several months earlier. The Peatwhistles had decided that he wouldn't be replaced, since they thought a butler was no longer appropriate for modern times, which James noted with some satisfaction, but decided that his views were best kept to himself on this occasion.

"Good morning, Peggy, how are you today? I haven't seen you for a while, have I?"

"Sadly no, Mr Young. I think you have been busy looking after Connor, my nephew's son." Peggy's voice lowered to a whisper. "You be careful, young sir. Sam Rivers is a very bad man and brings big trouble everywhere he goes. I've warned you before, and he's not finished yet."

"What do you mean, Peggy?" whispered James. "You do know he's dead, don't you?"

Peggy nodded her head and frowned, "I know, but he was once before, wasn't he?"

Peggy showed James into the 'breakfast room', but left James wondering how she knew that Sam was dead. James often wondered why Lotitia called this prettily decorated room 'the breakfast room', as she certainly never ate breakfast there. Lotitia usually started her day with a large gin and tonic, a cup of tea and a cigarette in her bedroom. He noted that the usually sprightly woman was now sitting in an upright chair, looking older and clearly in some pain. Lotitia appeared to read his thoughts.

"Hello James. Do please sit down. I will stay here, if you don't mind. It's the arthritis getting to me, Age I guess, I'm not as young as I was, what?"

Lotitia beckoned James to a comfortable chair, "I find an upright chair to be more comfortable at the moment, if that's what you're wondering, what? I've asked for some coffee and scones, I know you like them, and cook made some especially for you this morning."

James smiled and nodded, "That would be lovely. I'd hoped there would be some. Look, Lotitia, you are not going to like what I am about to tell you. It will be painful for you to hear, and I apologise before I start."

There was a tap at the door, and Peggy appeared carrying a tray containing a plate of scones, a large cup of coffee and a glass of what James assumed was a gin and tonic. Peggy quickly left the room.

Lotitia nodded, took a large sip from the glass and beckoned for James to continue.

"As you know, we have been looking after young Connor for a few weeks now. I know you have met him a few times."

"He's a lovely young boy. So bright too," nodded Lotitia.

"We are very concerned about him as it looks as if he would have to go into a children's home or be looked after by foster parents in Cornwall. Apparently, he has no other family who would be able to help. I have been thinking about adopting him myself."

Lotitia nodded and paused, "Well, that sounds like an eminently sensible solution for all concerned, what? I know you both like children, and frankly I can think of no one better. I am wondering why I should be alarmed, James? From what you have told me, this is something to be pleased about and does not concern me in the slightest, what?"

James continued, hesitantly, "Young Connor gave me a letter a few days ago. It was written by er, Sam, Sam Rivers."

James paused and took a large sip of coffee, and waited for some reaction.

"Sam Rivers? Did you say Sam Rivers?" Lady Lotitia glared with fury at James, and her bright blue eyes shone dangerously, in exactly the same way as Sam's eyes shone when he was angry or disturbed. James never had any doubts that Lotitia was Sam's birth mother, as he had seen those eyes flash dangerously before in different circumstances.

James nodded and took another sip of coffee.

"And may I ask what this letter said?"

James retold the contents of the letter, which he had in his pocket, but avoided showing it to the furious woman seated opposite. He told the story of his journey to Benidorm, Sam's death, and Sam's wishes for Connor. As he spoke, James sensed the elderly woman's anger, which she kept calmly under control, although her bright blue eyes continued to flash dangerously as he spoke. When he had finished, he paused and waited for an explosion of anger that surprisingly never came.

"Is he dead this time then?" Lotitia asked casually, after a lengthy pause and several gulps of liquid from the near empty glass.

"Yes, I believe so. I brought his ashes home with me. They are at the undertakers in Abbotsford. We thought we should have a funeral, for Connor's sake. Sam was his father, after all."

"Why didn't you throw them into the sea, what?" exclaimed Lotitia. "We dealt with his ashes once, and I'm certainly not going to mourn for that evil child of mine again."

"You have a grandchild, Lotitia. We need to consider him. He thought a lot of his father."

"Stuff and nonsense, James! He was a very evil man. Have you forgotten what he tried to do to me and

Toby? He nearly succeeded too. If it hadn't been for your quick thinking, we would all be dead. As for you, he made your life hell; he shot you and poor Prince! I shall never forget how much that dear dog of yours suffered. No, I want to forget him, as if he had never been born! As for Connor, I doubt very much that he is Sam's."

"That won't be possible, Lotitia. We have to consider Connor now. It's his life that we should be thinking about. He's only nine, and he deserves a chance in life. Please don't deny him that!"

James could see that there was about to be an outburst of rage from the angry woman, but instead he could see that she was gradually calming down, sipping her glass and thinking deeply. James decided that he would say no more for the time being and would focus upon buttering the warm scone before it got cold.

After what seemed to James to be a silence of several minutes, Lotitia stood up, rang the bell and waited for Peggy to reappear.

"Another G and T, Peggy. James, more coffee?"

James shook his head and continued to eat his scone. Peggy quickly reappeared and handed a rather larger glass than the first to Lady Lotitia.

When Peggy had gone, Lotitia sat down again with a deep sigh.

"Of course, you are right, James. You usually are when it comes to children. Yes, Connor must come first, but I want nothing to do with my son or his funeral, what? He is already dead to me. Despite this, I endorse your decision to adopt Connor. As I understand it, these things are difficult, as you are a homosexual, but I am sure that we can get around it with Sir Toby's clever lawyer getting involved, if needed. In some ways, this could work out better for you and Connor since, if Connor is Sam's son, then I am presumably Connor's only blood relative, which means that no one else will be able to have a claim on the boy. You do of course remember that Peggy is technically Sam's aunt, as she is Rita's sister, what?"

James nodded, "Do you think Peggy will be a problem, and will want to look after Connor herself?" asked James anxiously.

Lotitia shook her head, and gave a strained laugh. "Goodness me, of course not, she's too old and a bit batty, as you know well. Anyway, she dislikes children. She won't be a problem, I can assure you. I think you said that his Spanish mother is dead, and there are no other relatives on her side that know about Connor, what?"

"That is what I have been told by the Spanish lawyer who knew Sam well."

"Good, that should make it easier for all concerned, what? My indiscretions as a young woman are already generally well known by most of the village, and although the news of Sam's re-emergence and second death will cause yet more gossip and, I dare say, amusement, it is nothing that we haven't been through before. The news that Sam has a son who you intend to adopt will no doubt be a different story, what?"

James nodded thoughtfully, "Yes, I guess so. Do you think they won't approve of a gay man adopting Connor? Will this cause more trouble for you?"

Lotitia snapped, "Of course not, not in this village anyway. Everyone knows how good you are with children; they like you and Christian too. Woe betide anyone who says otherwise. No, I think the gossip will be around Connor, and questions will be asked whether he will he turn out to be his father's son. In your hands, James, I am sufficiently confident to suggest that hell would freeze over before that happened."

The old lady smiled before continuing. "No, you go ahead, we may all be in for a rough ride at first, but let's focus upon Connor's future, and not the demise of an evil, cunning and misguided man. Speaking of futures, I suggest that we immediately establish a trust fund for Connor, and I will put money in for the boy's future."

"I think Mr Carter is already doing this. You see, Connor seems to have been left a very large sum of money by his father, which has just been sent over from Spain."

"Ill-gotten gains, I can be certain of that. No, I want the boy to have access to genuine funds for a good start in life. Get your solicitor to set a fund up, James, and keep me informed, what?"

"I'll do that, of course. Now about the funeral ..."

"That's quite enough for one day, young man," snapped Lotitia as she determinedly strode out of the room, seemingly forgetting the pain that she had claimed to be in earlier.

Chapter 22

"No, no, no!" exclaimed James angrily. "We're not having this turned into some macabre spectacle. We are not using Connor in this way. I've never heard of anything so ridiculous, Jasmine!"

"But he'd look so cute walking up the church aisle carrying his father's urn. He could wear a small top hat and tails, just like they used to do with small boys in the old days. Or maybe he could wear one of those flat caps like Oliver Twist wore in that film. Hmm, no, I think the top hat and tails would be best..."

James couldn't believe what he was hearing, and Doris lifted up her eyes heavenwards, "That woman is just unbelievable," she muttered.

"No!" said James, sharply. "There will only be a few of us there anyway. Please let's keep the funeral short and simple. Do you understand what I am asking, Jasmine?"

"I wish we hadn't put Connor through this now," muttered James, attempting to squeeze into the trousers of a dark grey suit that he had last worn at Tristan's funeral three years earlier. "I should have scattered Sam's ashes from the cliffs overlooking Benidorm, and not brought them home. We wouldn't be having all this fuss if I had done that. Goodness knows what else Jasmine will come up with today!"

"No, I think you are right. Connor needs time to grieve properly, Jay. It will help to provide closure for him, and hopefully he can begin to move on again," said Christian, standing by the bedroom door, anxiously looking at his watch.

James nodded, "I just wish I had stopped the Rector from asking Connor to read that Bible passage. The boy is only nine for goodness sake. I'm surprised that he didn't have more sense than to ask him. One of us could have done it."

"Well, Connor said he was happy to do it, Jay. Both you and I have offered to do it for him, but he said that he wants to do something for his Dad."

James, Christian and Connor sat in the front pew of the church, with Connor between them. The beautiful village church shared the same golden sandstone as the rest of the village, as its fine features glowed in the bright sun streaming through the windows. They were soon joined by Doris and George, who sat next to James, followed by Lady Lotitia Peatwhistle, wearing the most enormous, and unfortunate, black hat, complete with black veil, who sat next to Christian. James felt sorry for anyone who would sit behind her, since they wouldn't be able to see a thing. James gave Lotitia a warm smile, and Lotitia whispered in reply.

"Yes, I know I said I wouldn't come, as I've already buried Sam's ashes once before, remember? I thought the villagers would think it strange, what? Anyway, I'm here for the boy; he is the one that matters now."

James nodded, "I think you've made the right decision. We appreciate you being with us, Lotitia."

They were soon joined by other mourners, Cedric, Anne Armstrong and other staff from the school made their presence quietly known to James and Christian, as they sat in the pews behind them. The new, young Rector, Finley Fender, greeted everyone with a smile or a handshake as they entered the church. James spotted Paula and Jasmine fluttering around the solid wooden table that held Sam's urn, adding the finishing touches to the flowers that surrounded it. Before he had sat down, Connor had insisted that he place Sam's Stetson on top of the urn, to which Jasmine was about to remove as soon as the boy had turned his back.

"Just leave it!" hissed James, in a tone that Jasmine had never heard before. For once, she looked shocked and promptly sat down.

As James had requested, the service was short and respectful. The congregation sang "All Things Bright and Beautiful," which Connor had suggested. There were then two prayers, followed by Connor reading a passage from the Bible. As Connor squeezed out of the pew, James rubbed his arm and Christian gave him a quick hug, "You will be great," he whispered.

Connor read the passage with clarity and meaning, and not usually associated with a nine-year-old boy. James swallowed hard, as he tried hard to stop his tears, whilst Christian suddenly discovered that he had to tie his shoelaces and disappeared beneath the pew to do so. Doris had tears running down her face, whilst Lady Lotitia snorted loudly into a white, lace-trimmed handkerchief. When Connor had finished reading, he turned towards Sam's urn, bowed reverently and walked back to his seat. James held Connor's hand as he squeezed between him and Christian, "Well done, your Dad would be so proud of you. Christian and I are too."

At the end of the service, and as they turned to walk out of the church, following Sam's urn that was carried slowly and respectfully by Paula, James noticed that the church was completely full, and there were even villagers standing at the rear of the church, since they were unable to find a seat. James was deeply moved and whispered to Christian, "I just cannot believe it. I think most of the village has turned out to support us."

James, Christian, Connor, accompanied by Doris and Lady Lotitia stood by the small grave. The Reverend Fender said another prayer, as Paula and Jasmine together gently placed Sam's urn into the grave. Connor stepped forward and dropped a red rose into the grave, and in a clear voice said, "I love you, Dad. Goodbye," before he turned and re-joined James and Christian, who held each of his hands in reassurance.

As the mourners stood in prayerful silence around Sam's grave, James felt that were being closely watched. He looked around, but could see no one. He sensed a sudden chill, just as if someone had just walked over his own grave.

Chapter 23

James, Christian and Connor were the last to leave the graveside, as Doris and Lady Lotitia had sensibly and discreetly left them to join the other mourners who were heading towards the Manor House.

"Well done, Connor," began Christian, still holding his hand. "You were very brave today."

"I told you I could be brave, didn't I?" replied Connor, looking up at Christian.

"You certainly did, young man. Just remember that you can come here any time to remember your Dad. We know he's not really here, but it is a special place that you can come and think of him and maybe say a prayer."

"I would like that," agreed Connor. "Who were all those people that came to the service?"

"They are your new extended family, Connor. They are people who you may not know yet, but they will help and care for you in the days ahead. They are our friends and are mostly from Prior's Hill."

In what was the old ballroom, which was now renamed the 'Music Room', Lady Lotitia had arranged a magnificent after-funeral spread. Much to her usual cook's disgust, she had brought in outside caterers who provided plates of delicious looking sandwiches, cakes, sausage rolls and all manner of treats. At the far end of the room, there was a small bar, with staff busily handing out glasses of wine, beer and fruit juice.

"My goodness," exclaimed James, "I thought we would only need to cater for a dozen people at most. Last week, I thought we could do this at Lavender Cottage, but I'm pleased we didn't. Lady Lotitia has been so generous, hasn't she? She's insisted about arranging and paying for everything."

Lady Lotitia was clearly enjoy the moment. It might be an after-funeral party, but she loved all manner of social gatherings. An event such as this, with people whom she actually liked, rather than barely tolerated, was just what she enjoyed most about her position as Lady of the Manor. Most importantly, no one other than James, mentioned Sam Rivers or his demise by name; they knew better than to attract Lady Lotitia's wrath.

James went over to thank her, and was grateful that the large, black hat had been removed. She listened to James, and then brushed his thanks aside.

"It's the least that I could do. I just cannot help thinking about the poor boy. What? I like Connor, he is such a sensible chap. Yes, I know he is supposed to be Sam's son, but that is not the boy's fault, and I have my doubts about that anyway, what? I want nothing to do with him as a grandmother, but only as your son. I know that he is in good hands with you and Christian."

"Lotitia, I have one question the has been troubling me. It is something that you briefly mentioned the other day, and you have just mentioned it again now."

"What might that be?"

"You said that you had doubts that Connor is Sam's son. Why do you say that?"

"Because he looks nothing like Sam," snapped Lotitia. "For a start, yes, he has blonde hair, but not the colour of straw like Sam. He doesn't have the same blue, often cold eyes that Sam had, and that I sometimes see in myself. As for physique, even Doris commented the other day when Christian and Connor were in the swimming pool that the boy appears stunted and awkward in his movements. I put that down to poor diet and lack of exercise, but he is not doubt jointed or at all athletic like his father."

"Yes, but I have his birth certificate and Sam's letter says that …"

"Yes, I appreciate all that, but it doesn't mean it's true. The more I think about it, the more I am convinced that Connor is not Sam's son. I just sense it James. If I am right, and I think I am, we should all be very grateful that no spawn of that monster exists. You mark my words, James, I would put money on it."

James nodded, "Well, you may be right. Everything about Sam turns out to be a lie. We are just going to focus upon Connor."

"By the way," interrupted Lady Lotitia, deftly changing the subject as she opened the small, decorative handbag that she was carrying, and thrust an envelope into James' hand. "I have thought about it, and I am very happy to be a trustee of Connor's trust fund, and Sir Toby and I would like to make this contribution to start it off. What?"

"There really is no need, Lotitia," began James, "Connor is actually quite well off, because …"

"Nonsense! All young people could do with a spot of extra cash. Just give him a few extra treats, James. Send him to public school, buy him a car or something when he is a bit bigger. You'll know the sort of thing. By the way, where is Prince? You should have brought him along, as he would have enjoyed it. Never mind, I will get cook to prepare a 'doggy bag' of a few treats for him, as there will be plenty of left-overs, I'm sure. Dogs are so much more pleasant that children, don't you think, what?"

With a final flourish, Lady Lotitia headed towards a group of villagers who were admiring a very large floral display in one of the large bay windows.

"All home grown," she announced loudly.

James finally realised that he would never understand her.

James, Christian, Doris, George and Connor walked back to their cars, relieved that the funeral had gone as well as it could. Doris walked with Connor, holding his hand, whilst James and Christian walked behind reflecting upon the busy day.

"Yes, it did go well, and I think it was well worth doing for Connor. As you said, Jay, it is somewhere where he can go and think about his Dad. I was also pleased to see him chatting to Anne Armstrong. I think you said that he would be in her class. She's nice, Connor will like her."

"That's right, and I think it is already mutual. Anne seems very impressed with him, particularly since he's been telling her all about the Charles Dickens novels that his has read, and his views on 'Lord of the Flies'. She's worried that he will soon be on 'War and Peace', which she says she has never read," laughed James. "I think young Connor will keep us all on our toes."

"I was really moved to see so many villagers in the church, Jay. They didn't have to come, and particularly because most have never met Connor. I'm sure that they must remember all the bad things that Sam Rivers did when he lived in the village. Admittedly, some may have turned up because they were just curious, or wanted to make sure that Sam really was dead this time, or maybe they were just after Lotitia's fine spread afterwards, but I genuinely do believe that they were there to support the three of us. They have all been so kind to us; I really do feel that we belong here, and that these people have become our very large family."

James nodded. You remember that several weeks ago, when I was working far too hard and you were worried about me? Well, I told you then that I didn't want to leave Prior's Hill. This is why, Chris. These people have become our family. I am so happy here, and now that Connor is with us, I feel that it is complete. I'm just so happy!"

Christian nodded and smiled. He knew exactly what James meant as the small group walked together, bathed in the remaining warmth of the sun.

Chapter 24

"Right then, I'm off," shouted Christian to James, who was still upstairs getting ready to start the day. Connor was already downstairs playing with Prince, who had just had a brief walk and had already eaten his breakfast.

"My goodness, you are up bright and early today, Chris!" exclaimed James, as he entered the kitchen. "It's going to be a long drive and then a long meeting, I guess."

Christian nodded, "I guess I'll be back late too. Have your meal, don't wait for me. I'll get something later, if I feel like it."

"Can I come with you?" asked Connor, enthusiastically. "I've still got some time before I start school next week. I could keep you company. Perhaps Prince could come as well, and I could take him for a walk while I'm waiting for you?"

"I would like nothing more," replied Christian, "but it's going to be a very long and boring day, and I'll be home long past your bedtime."

"Anyway, I have plans for you today, young man," laughed James. "You've obviously forgotten that you are supposed to help Mrs Armstrong and myself to sort out books for the new library."

Connor's eyes lit up. "Oh yes, I had forgotten; I was looking forward to doing that."

"Well, that's sorted then. I'll see you both very soon. Have a good day," said Christian, as he closed the cottage door before Prince could decide to join him.

Connor spent what he considered to be a most enjoyable day sorting books and carrying them to the new library with James and Mrs Armstrong. Later during the morning, Doris joined them, bearing a tray of delicious looking cakes and mugs of coffee, as well as some juice for Connor.

"Hello, Doris. What are you doing here?" asked Anne. "We don't start until next week."

"Good morning, Anne. I'm just completing the new registers, as well as making some payments before the new term begins. The new extension looks lovely, doesn't it. I've just had a quick look. Are you pleased with it, James?"

"Well, I was until I spotted some of the paintwork …" began James.

"Don't get him started, Doris," laughed Anne. "Cedric and I have already spotted it, and the builders have promised to do it again before the children return."

"They better had," mumbled James, "I've had enough of all the mess and general chaos. It's been going on for weeks, but I have to say they have cleaned up quite well. Cedric and the cleaners have made a really good job too. The school seems to sparkle, and we are almost ready for another busy term. I'm really looking forward to it."

"Are you looking forward to starting school too?" asked Anne, as Connor entered the small library, carrying another pile of books. "You really shouldn't be carrying so many books at one time, Connor, you could hurt yourself."

"I don't mind, Mrs Armstrong, but thank you. I know I'm a bit small, but I am quite strong really. Yes, I am very excited about starting school in your class next week. Will we be doing algebra? I like algebra, and I'm quite good at it."

Anne looked a little startled, "Erm, yes, possibly Connor. If we don't get to that, I'll prepare some for you to work on with your Dad at home."

"Gee, thanks Anne," grumbled James. "I hate algebra. Don't you encourage Mrs Armstrong with that Connor! Right, let's get these books into some kind of order."

"Will we be putting them into alphabetical order, or using the Dewey Classification System, Mr Young?" asked Connor, enthusiastically. "I hope we can use Dewey, as I was used to it when I went to the library. Did you know that someone called Melvil Dewey invented it in the 18 somethings? It's the most popular library classification system in the world."

"No, I don't think I knew that, Connor, but it is a very useful system. They use it in the Abbotsford Library. We'll visit it next week, if you like."

"Did you visit the library often, Connor?" asked Anne.

"No, not very often, because Dad said it was dangerous. He used to bring lots of books home for me instead, but I did visit it a few times. I love being in the library."

"Why dangerous? asked Anne, looking puzzled. Connor didn't answer, leaving the room to collect another pile of books.

Chapter 25

Christian set off on the long journey to Bodmin. Although James knew part of the reason for his journey, he hadn't told him everything that he had planned to do that day. James was still coming to terms with all that had happened to him in Benidorm, and the readjustment that they were all making to suddenly becoming fathers. Christian didn't want to burden him with more concerns.

Christian had fallen for James the first time that he had met both him and Tristan during their proposed purchase of Lavender Cottage. He quickly became friends with both young men, and did his best to support James following Tristan's untimely death. Over time, Christian's caring support for James turned into a love that Christian could only dream of. His own loveless upbringing by a bullying father and weak mother made Christian even more determined to ensure that his relationship with James would be happy and supportive. Christian was also determined that Connor, whom he now began to regard as their son, would grow up within a warm and loving family.

He thought back to the time when he was disowned by his parents, when they discovered that he was gay. As a bewildered seventeen-year-old, Christian had travelled to London to find work where he was groomed and abused by older men. It was Peter, his loyal friend from childhood, who rescued him from serious trouble and introduced him to his Uncle Frank and Aunt Eleanor. It was this couple who generously took Christian into their home and treated him as their own son, and gave him the loving family that he had never had. It was also thanks to Uncle Frank that Christian was introduced to life as an estate agent, and given an opportunity to join the Abbotsford branch of the estate agency, Whitney and Walker, which is where Christian first met James and Tristan. He smiled as he remembered Uncle Frank's mantra that he had drummed into Christian as a trainee estate agent, "Be friendly, be honest and be professional." These were words that Christian valued highly, and tried to apply to life in general, as well as his professional life. Christian's parents were now dead and although he had a younger sister, Patricia, he had not seen her for many years.

Christian was concerned about James, and he had been for some time. The re-occurring nightmares that James had told Christian about were troubling, particularly as the detail was always the same. Even more worrying was that the events in Benidorm seemed to parody those nightmares. On the positive side, Christian knew that James always worked far too hard, and was pleased that adopting Connor was beginning to change Jim for the better. He had hardly talked about school and, for once, had delegated much of the supervision to Anne Armstrong, his loyal deputy.

He reflected upon the funeral. Christian was surprised by the number of people that had appeared at the church to show their support. He knew that James and he were well liked in the village; James had helped and advised so many of the parents to deal with serious issues in their personal lives that often affected their children. James was well respected for his ability as an excellent teacher, but as someone who worked hard to defend the interests of their children, the school and wider village community.

Connor had already changed their lives for the better, but Christian was saddened to see the impact that the last few weeks had had upon the small boy. He and Connor were developing a good relationship, and Connor seemed to regard Christian as a much older 'big brother', and he would talk and share things that troubled him with Christian that he had not shared with James.

Christian had been very angry about what he had heard when he and Connor were making lunch together early that week. Connor liked sandwiches and enjoyed making them. However, it appeared that this was mainly what he had lived on when he was on his own in the farm cottage, and often for many weeks at a time. Sam had bought a large supply of tinned food, as well as a second-hand freezer that he stocked up with food for Connor when he was working in Benidorm. Sadly, the freezer had broken down shortly after Sam had left, and the food had melted. Conor had also told him that the bottled gas for the old stove had run out and he was not strong enough to fit the new gas bottle on to the adapter, and so he could not heat any food.

Sam had warned Connor never to leave Hope Cottage, because "bad men were after them", but accepted that Connor would occasionally go to the old farm building to play with the newly-born kittens. Connor had returned in tears one day shortly after the kittens were born, as the farmer had told him that one of them was "a little runt" and that he would have to drown him. Connor had begged him not to do this and promised the farmer that he would look after the helpless kitten himself. When Sam was away, Connor had bottle-fed the tiny scrap of life, and brought him back to the cottage where the kitten rapidly gained in strength.

When Sam returned home from Benidorm, he was angry when he saw the kitten and said that they couldn't afford to look after him. They would be moving again soon anyway, and it wasn't fair on the kitten, as they would have to leave him behind. Sam made Connor take him back to the farmer and Connor had been very upset. Connor took the kitten, Mittens, as he called him, back to the barn where the kitten seemed to settle and play with the other kittens. He would go to see the kitten each day to check he was alright. It was during these visits that the farmer's wife would see him entering the barn. She would usually make him a sandwich or some soup. Connor had told Christian that the farmer's wife began to ask him many questions about going to school, and Connor pretended that he had a problem with his hearing and didn't always hear what was being said to him.

Christian shook his head in anger when he had heard how hard it had been for Connor to keep Sam's secrets, and the way that he had been treated. Connor had been left for weeks on his own; his only companions being the kittens and a huge pile of books that Sam would occasional bring back for him. Conor told him that once someone had arrived from the school and had knocked on the door and they had to pretend not to be in. They had posted a letter under the door about Connor having to go to school, which Sam had torn up in anger.

Connor told Christian that sometimes men would arrive at the cottage; they spoke in a "funny way" and were often shouting at Sam. Sam was usually expecting them and they would arrive late at night when it was dark. Connor was always sent to bed, but he could hear them talking for many hours, and in an accent and language that he didn't understand.

Christian asked Connor about the old woman who was supposed to be Connor's grandmother, but was really Sam in disguise. Connor had talked about this with pride and he appeared to be very proud that Sam was such an accomplished actor. He told Christian that Sam's recreation of his grandmother was exactly as she had been when she was alive. Following the death of his mother, his grandmother had brought Connor up, and he missed her. Connor found it comforting when Sam dressed up as his grandmother, which Christian thought to be troubling.

When Christian arrived in Bodmin, he parked the car and went immediately to an old pub, called 'The Hangman's Rope', which is where he planned to meet a colleague who worked at the one of the sister branches of the estate agency.

"Hello Christian, I'm over here," came a voice from the end of the bar. Christian waved in acknowledgement and walked over to the far corner where he greeted his friend; an older man sporting an impressive greying beard.

"Hello Patrick, it's good to see you again. How long ago were you working in Abbotsford? Let me get some drinks ordered."

"Oh, it must be four or five years now, Christian. You started there, young and inexperienced. I gather that you are now the branch manager; you have done really well for yourself. I am told that your branch is a very successful business, and it is mostly down to your efforts."

"Thanks, Patrick. Much of that is thanks to you. You trained me, remember?"

Patrick nodded, "Yes, I do. I enjoyed my time there and we got on well didn't we? Apart from that cock up you made with that strange woman's house, I forget the detail. I think you double sold it, didn't you?"

Christian laughed, "I can laugh about it now, but both buyers were very angry, weren't they? They threatened to take the company to court. I thought I was going to be sacked."

"You very nearly were, but we managed to sort it out," laughed Patrick. "Well, young man, what have you been doing, other than working?"

"Well, I am now a father," announced Christian proudly, and proceeded to tell Patrick a shortened version of the last few weeks and, in particular to share his concerns about Connor and his father, Sam.

Patrick listened carefully as he sipped his beer. "Well, you asked me to make some enquiries about the cottage and its occupants, 'Hope Cottage', I think you said. Well, I asked a good friend of mine who is a constable at the station here, Peter Steggles. We're in the pub's darts team together. Well, Peter said that an old woman and her grandson live there. They haven't been there long. Trent, the farmer who owns the place, said a young man visits her sometimes, who he assumes is the old woman's son. The boy doesn't go to school, but he thinks social services are on the case. Apparently, the boy has a hearing problem."

Christian nodded, "This is very helpful, thank you."

Patrick took another large gulp of his beer and continued, "Peter also said that he thought something a bit strange was going on there. Apparently, there have been visits from strangers very late at night recently, according to Trent. They stay very late too. One night there was a loud crash that woke Trent. He suspected that someone was trying to steal some of his brand-new farm machinery, so he went outside to investigate. There were two burly men in the car and they had hit one of the gate posts as they were trying to leave. One of the men got out of the car, apologised and offered to pay for the damage. According to Trent, the man was foreign and had a strange foreign accent, which he didn't recognise."

"Well, maybe they were just visiting the old woman," commented Christian.

"Maybe, but according to Peter there have been enquiries from the London force asking whether there have been any foreigners visiting Hope Cottage. That's all he knows. It may be something or nothing, Christian, but you did ask me to find out anything that I could. I'll let you know if I hear anything else."

Christian left Bodmin just as it was beginning to pour with rain and drove to 'Hope Cottage'. It looked deserted from the gateway, but as he got closer he was puzzled to find that the windows had not been boarded-up as James had been told. He got out of the car, in the pouring rain, and peered through the dirty windows. It looked untidy, but it was exactly as he remembered it. The old chair that the woman had been sitting in was still there, Connor's table and chair, two unmade beds, and an old, dirty-looking stove. Again, Christian recalled that James had been told by social services that everything had been removed, because the cottage was going to be refurbished and let as a holiday cottage. It all looked exactly the same as when they had last visited.

Puzzled, Christian left the cottage and walked the short way to the farmer's house. He knocked on the door, which was opened by Trent. Trent, a jolly-looking, ruddy faced, older man, shook his hand and insisted that he come inside.

"It's pouring out there. You look as if you are soaked through. Would you like a cup of tea to warm yourself up?"

"That's very kind of you Trent, but I have a long journey and must be on my way. I'll dry off in the car."

"Just as you like. As we agreed on the phone, I've put the kitten in a box. He's had some food and a drink, so will be alright for the journey. I think the boy calls him Mittens. It was a poor little scrap, but the boy looked after him very well, and he's now quite strong. I think he'll survive."

"Thank you so much, Trent. Mittens will make a sad little boy very happy."

"Pleased to help. He's a nice little lad, doesn't say much mind, but wife says he's got a hearing problem. We were very worried about him. Wife used to feed him when she saw him, but we reported it to social services. I can't understand people leaving a kid like that on their own."

"Yes, I agree," nodded Christian. "He's being well looked after now. Tell me, did anyone ever come to see them?"

Trent thought for a moment, stroking his chin. "There was a young man around sometimes, who we think was her son, but he never stayed long."

"Anyone else?"

"We had a scare one night when we heard a loud crash. I thought someone was trying to steal my new tractor. It turned out to be two foreigners who hit the gate post when they were leaving."

"Did they damage anything?" asked Christian.

"No, just the gate post and the side of their car. An expensive beast that looked, a Mercedes, I think. Why do you ask?"

"I'm just interested because Connor said they never had visitors."

"Oh, they did. Those men visited several times. I recognised the car. Spoke funny though, sounded Russian to me, but I can't be sure. I remember thinking it sounded like on those spy films."

"Well, thank you again, Trent. It's time I got Mittens home. There's a small boy who will burst with excitement when he sees him."

"Good luck to the lad, Christian. I'm sure Mittens will do well in the boy's care."

Chapter 26

James was thinking that it was time for Connor to go to bed, when he heard the cottage gate click. Prince, who had been asleep on the sofa, gave a volley of barking, leapt off the comfortable sofa, and headed towards the kitchen door.

"That's Christian, I'm sure. We'd better see if he would like us to reheat some dinner for him, or maybe make him a sandwich. You could do that Connor, if you like?"

Connor smiled, "I like making sandwiches."

The kitchen door opened, and in bounded Christian, with Prince barking enthusiastically around him. Christian looked very pleased with himself, and was carrying a large cardboard box.

"Hello folks," he announced, giving James a big hug and kiss, and ruffling Connor's hair. "Have you missed me? What have you been up to today, Connor?"

"I've been helping Mr Young and Mrs Armstrong with some books in the new library. What have you got in that box, Christian?"

"It's a surprise for you, Connor. "That's where I have been all day. Take a look inside."

Prince was already sniffing the outside of the box. Connor carefully opened the lid of the box and peered inside.

"No, it can't be!" he exclaimed, "It's a kitten. It's, it's Mittens." Connor lifted the young cat carefully out of the box and held him in his arms. Prince looked away and sat in his bed, looking with disgust at this new invasion into his territory.

The young boy grinned broadly, and stroked the bewildered kitten. James and Christian had never seen Connor look so happy in the short time that they had known him.

Mittens was a handsome black kitten, with four white socks and a white chest and stomach. He was clearly used to Connor and looked perfectly happy in his arms.

"How can this be? I left Mittens in Cornwall with the farmer. Dad wouldn't let me keep him."

"We know," began James. "We know that Mittens was a great friend of yours in Cornwall and that the farmer gave him to you. We thought you deserved a treat after all the sad things that have happened recently. Christian spoke to the farmer a few days ago, and he said that you could have him. That's why Christian has been away all day and didn't want you to go with him. It's a surprise."

"I understand now," laughed Connor, "Thank you, thank you so much!" He then looked very concerned. "We don't have any food for him. We haven't got a bed ready for him or anything," began Connor, anxiously.

"Don't worry, Connor," said Christian. "James has solved that. He has already bought a small bed, a blanket, litter tray, special kitten food and two or three toys for Mittens. We thought you would like to go shopping in Abbotsford tomorrow to choose one or two special toys for him. Kittens need to play a lot, and I am sure that you will help with that."

"Can I also hold him?" asked James, anxious to greet the new arrival.

"Yes, of course," replied Connor, gently passing Mittens to James.

"He really is a beautiful kitten, Connor, and I can see why you call him Mittens. We will take him to the vet tomorrow to get him checked, and to have the injections that will keep him healthy. Are you happy to take responsibility for him? The deal means that you are responsible for feeding and playing with him, as well as cleaning out his litter tray! By the way, is he a boy or a girl, do you know?"

Connor laughed and shook his head, "No, and the farmer said he didn't have a clue either. That's why I chose the name Mittens, as I thought it would be a good name for a boy or a girl cat. Anyway, I expect the vet will tell us tomorrow. They have ways of finding out, you know," he added wisely.

"By the way, you also still have to take care of Prince," added Christian, as he cuddled the bewildered dog.

Later that night, as they were getting ready for bed, James hugged Christian.

"You've made our little boy so very happy. Thank you for driving all that way on your own. What a wonderful surprise it has been for him. I've never seen him look so happy. It was well worth the effort, wasn't it?"

Christian nodded and yawned, "Yes, it was well worth it. I was surprised how quickly Mittens settled in tonight too. He is a beautiful kitten, isn't he? I thought we would have a very bad night with a new kitten in the house. I see that Prince has joined us back on our bed tonight though."

"Yes," laughed James, stroking the tired dog, "I guess the downside of this arrangement is that he will once again take up more of the bed that we do. By the way, did you manage to check out 'Hope Cottage'?"

"Yes," replied Christian, looking puzzled. "I'm sure that you told me that the social worker friend of yours, Sarah Tibbles, said that the cottage had been boarded up, and was going to be completely renovated and let to holidaymakers."

James got into bed, "Yes, that's what she said. One of her colleagues had been to check the property and said it was completely empty."

"Well, someone's not telling the truth, Jay. When I checked, the cottage was not boarded up, it looked just as we had left it. I looked through the windows and all the furniture was still there, grandmother's chair, beds, Connor's desk and chair, and that old gas stove. Everything was just as we had left it."

Chapter 27

A friendly observer with a spirit of warmth and generosity would no doubt gain great pleasure from looking at the contented, domestic scene through the open curtained window of Lavender Cottage. There were two young men, obviously in love, sitting on the sofa together with their large, much loved dog who was snoring loudly big a large dinner. A small boy was happily playing with his new friend, a young kitten, on the cosy rug in front of the fireplace.

James was reading the latest edition of the Times Educational Supplement, a paper that he usually read avidly each week, but had not even glanced at during the long summer holiday. He reflected upon how unusual it was for him to be detached from school. He now had other priorities in his life, and he was rather enjoying it.

Christian was leafing through the pages of a model railway magazine, glancing at the adverts for accessories that would enhance the train set that they had set up together at the far end of the living room. He was wondering about getting an additional train, and would show Connor the one that he had in mind at bedtime.

"Jay? I've got an idea," announced Christian.

James put down his paper, and looked at his partner, questioningly.

"Go on, I'm listening."

"Well, you remember when we first moved here, we said we would build an extension. We reckoned we couldn't afford it, but since Frank and Eleanor and the Peatwhistles together bought the cottage for us, I'm sure we can afford it. Now Connor is with us, we need an extra bedroom, and I thought we could build one for us, with an ensuite bathroom attached. Connor could then have our room, which would give him more room for his train set and all the extensions he's planning."

"Oh, that's a good idea," exclaimed Connor, excitedly, "I like the sound of this!"

James nodded and laughed, "Well, I've been thinking exactly the same thing. Connor's room is fine as a guest room, but not for all the railway extensions you two are planning. We can kit it out properly, and Connor can help to plan it. He will need a desk for all his homework, as well," James added, looking seriously at Connor, and winked.

"Great! I've also been thinking, Jay. Can we ask Aunt Eleanor and Uncle Frank to join us for Christmas? I miss them so much, and they cannot wait to meet Connor. They will be his kind of honorary grandparents."

James nodded, "Funnily enough, I've been thinking about that as well. We haven't managed to see them this summer and I know they get lonely at Christmas. I know the new extension won't be ready by then, but Doris does bed and breakfast, so I'm sure they could sleep there and spend the Christmas and New Year period with us. I think Doris and George would like that too."

"They can have my room," interrupted Connor, "I can easily sleep down here with Prince and Mittens."

James laughed, "You mean where Prince is supposed to sleep, in his basket by the radiator? We know he sleeps on your bed with Mittens, Connor! No, you stay where you are, but we will find somewhere comfortable for Eleanor and Frank to stay too, I promise you. Thank you for offering though. You are very thoughtful."

"How soon can we get on with the extension, do you think, Jay?" asked Christian, sounding very excited.

"I'd like it tomorrow, Chris," laughed James. "You know me. Look, I never thought I'd say this, but those builders at school are actually quite good. I know that we've had our differences, but how about getting a rough quote from them? I can also ask Tony, the architect for some advice, if you like."

"I like the sound of that, Jay. Yes, by all means, better the devils we know. Once we know a rough cost, I'll have a word with the bank."

Connor was happily sprawled out on the large, fluffy circular rug in front of the fireplace, with Mittens jumping on and off his stomach, as he tried to catch the toy mouse that Connor was holding. Connor giggled as the young cat ducked and dived, and finally caught the toy mouse. He paused and looked seriously at James.

"Mr Young?"

"Yes, Connor," replied James, putting down his paper again.

"Am I an orphan?"

James thought for a moment, "Well, biologically, yes, I guess you are, Connor, because both your mother and father have died, but that's not the whole story."

Connor looked quizzically at James, "What do you mean?"

"Well, Christian and I are both orphans like you, because our parents have died. It has happened to you much earlier than it should have done, which is very sad and should not have happened. Even though the three of us are orphans, we are not really orphans, because we have each other. We have created a family together of you, Christian, myself, Prince and now Mittens. Do you see what I mean?"

"You are adopting me, aren't you?"

"Yes, Connor. We are both adopting you, but you have to be registered to only me at the moment, as that is the law. It's going to take some time, but it means that you will have two Dads to look after you."

Connor nodded, "You said that my name is Carlos Connor Rivers-Sanchez, didn't you?"

James nodded, "Yes, Connor, you are half Spanish and half British. You are a very fortunate boy to be what they call a dual national, because it gives you more choices when you get older. Rivers is your real Dad's name, and Sanchez is your mother's name."

Connor thought for a moment, "In that case, when you have adopted me, can I change my name to Carlos Connor Young-Trill?" He giggled, "That sounds funny, does it?"

"I like the sound of that!" exclaimed Christian, putting down his magazine. "You can't go wrong with a Trill in your name!"

James laughed, "Yes, I like it too, but Rivers is your biological Dad's name. Don't you think you should keep it in his memory? Maybe think about this again when you are a bit older? Anyway, I think Connor Rivers is a much easier name for your new friends at school to understand, don't you?"

Connor nodded, and continued playing with Mittens. He looked up again at Christian.

Christian?"

"Yes, Connor?"

"May I call you Papa instead of Christian?"

Christian leant forward, grabbed the small boy and hugged him.

"I would like nothing more, Connor! It would be an honour for me if you call me Papa, but what are you going to do about James?"

Connor grinned and looked at James.

"Mr Young?"

"Yes, Connor?"

"May I please call you Dad?"

Anyone with a spirit of generosity and warmth would gain huge pleasure from observing this scene, but what if the friendly observer is someone malevolent, angry and intent upon doing harm?

Printed in Great Britain
by Amazon